Heir Presumptive

Tyra Davidson

AOS Publishing, 2024
Copyright © 2024 Tyra Davidson

ISBN: 978-1-998662-13-5

Cover Design: Chanelle Poupart

Visit AOS Publishing's website:
www.aospublishing.com

For my mother, Kate,
the first to tell me I could write my own books.

For Adrian, who told me the stories
that formed the basis of my own writing.

For Rebecca,
an unfailing source of support and steadfast companion in life.

Chapter One

Dead leaves crunched under the weight of booted feet, though the steps were light and careful. The young lady walking through the woods seemed to be expecting something to be lurking beneath the foliage, as she repeatedly shuffled the leaves with pointed toes before committing to putting her foot down. She made her way between the trees in this tentative manner, waist-length brown hair swinging in its plait.

Despite her cautious behaviour, the girl, Eleri, did not appear frightened of the woods, as she hummed a cheerful tune as she walked, sometimes singing snatches of songs under her breath. There was a sword hanging off her belt, but she only touched it if it was tangled in some branches. The forest itself was old growth, with the trees half bare and bright orange towering high over the lithe figure. Autumnal berries, heather, and gorse provided scattered pops of colour against the dull browns of the waning season.

Soon enough, Eleri came to a break in the trees, where years of human use had worn the grass away from the centre of the clearing, in an almost perfect circle. This opening was largely empty except for a large oak tree at the far end from her. Eleri picked her way over the brambles and thorns at the edge of the clearing, which seemed to have doubled their efforts in growing to compensate for the lack of greenery other than grass beyond. The ground in the clearing was also devoid of saplings, which was strange given the obvious age of the tree. It gave the clearing a strangely manicured appearance.

The first thing Eleri did was walk a quick loop of the clearing. Then, having not seen anything that gave cause for immediate concern, she unclipped her little embroidered leather pack from her belt, dropped it near a beech, and turned her attention to the interior of the clearing.

There were a variety of marks made in the dirt. Plenty of footprints, both from Eleri's quick check and many others, were pressed into the dirt. A large circle filled with intersecting lines was imprinted into the soil, almost like the aftermath of a burn. Other symbols, some drawn on the ground with a stick and some with differently coloured chalks and powders, both overlapped and lay under the circle. It was difficult to see what these coloured lines were, as they were frequently faded or wiped away in places.

Eleri crept around the circle, sometimes crouching down to scrutinise certain bits of it, a thoughtful frown on her face. Although she was not a mage, and therefore unlikely to reactivate the circle, it was better to be safe than sorry, especially in such a magic-heavy location. It was entirely possible someone had come to profane this pilgrimage site and left a nasty surprise for the next visitor.

It was clear the burnt circle had been used for a ritual of greater power than the others. Perhaps the mage responsible had needed the magic here to power their ritual, unable to do so alone. Mossy rocks stood at key points, markings drawn on them in a dried brown liquid. There was still a lingering feeling of *something* in the air, like a distant storm, staticky along Eleri's arms. It was also different from the usual ambient feeling in the clearing, which felt wearier and more distant. The aura emanating from the circle almost seemed to overpower that of the great tree at the end of the clearing—the reason Eleri had come.

Eleri returned to her pack and retrieved a small cloth bound book. It was raggedy, with little slips of paper sticking out at all angles. With practised gestures, she flipped through the pages, occasionally glancing up at the runes around her, as if comparing them to the notes. Finally, with a sharp and satisfied nod to herself, she snapped the book closed. Eleri strode across the clearing to the great tree, paying the circle no mind.

The tree towered above her and dwarfed many of the other trees around the clearing. It was clearly an old tree, with the bark cracked and peeling, the branches thick and clustered near the apex. One side of the base had a strange, knotted texture, as if the tree had once had to grow around something no longer there. The hollow left by this made a perfect divot for sitting. Eleri rested her forehead against the massive trunk. The tree *felt* ancient as well. Something about it projected an aura of being old and tired, the creaking of the branches in the wind almost like an old man groaning.

She'd been here once before, as a small girl holding tightly to her mother's skirts, hoping desperately not to be left behind. Then, the tree had seemed old in a friendly way, the way other children had described grandfathers, a kindly figure ready to dispense sweets and advice. Now, the tree seemed old in the way a decrepit rope bridge over a cavern was old—run-down and waiting for the end.

For the first time since arriving, she stood completely still. Her forehead was still pressed against the bark of the tree, and she took a deep breath, inhaling the forest scent. Without all her flitting back and forth, it became apparent that the world around her was too quiet. The clearing was devoid of the joyful chirping of birds, the wind didn't whistle through the branches, and no insect could be heard in the vacuum left behind. A sense of unease hung heavily in the air, making the skin at the back of Eleri's neck prickle.

With slow, deliberate movements, Eleri raised her head, blue eyes surreptitiously taking in her surroundings. She expected to see a predator skulking along the edges of the clearing, some person or beast hunting her for their own reasons. But there was no sign of life beyond that of the foliage around her. It was as if every other living thing not rooted in the ground had been sucked into some other dimension. It felt like some part of Eleri had been taken, too, leaving a punched-out, hollow feeling in her chest.

Even breathing felt sacrilegious, like it was a reminder that Eleri was still there, despite whatever had taken the life from the clearing. Nevertheless, Eleri took as deep a breath as possible to remind herself that she still could. There were times, especially when she was younger, that breathing was hard for her. Her chest would get tight, what air she could bring in never felt like enough, and when it was severe, she'd cough or wheeze. Every time, Eleri would get a sense of wrongness. There was something wrong now, too, but this time it was different. Instead of something being wrong with Eleri, there was something wrong with the world itself.

This strange new feeling left her staggered. Eleri half collapsed into the hollow of the tree, empty and breathless, ignoring the creaking of the wood. It felt sturdy enough to sit in, and being tucked away inside of the hollow almost provided a respite from the emptiness outside it. There was a small spark of—life, power, something, whatever had been stolen from the world at large, that remained with the tree.

Absentmindedly, Eleri started to pick out the leaves and twigs that had gotten stuck in her hair. The branches of tree and tall shrubs had caught her hair and tugged it, either sticking in the plait or pulling strands loose. It gave Eleri a bit of an unkempt look and made the blue ribbons she used to keep any stray hair away from the sides of her face lopsided. Oddly, there was nothing from the great tree, despite how she had walked through the branches many times as she circled it. Eleri was small, but even then, the top of her head had brushed the lowest of the tree's branches. Yet there were no oak leaves or twigs to be removed, nor were any of the scratches on her arms from the mighty oak.

As she ran her hands down her plait, smoothing it out now that it was debris free, Eleri started to hum softly. She reclined further into the embrace of the great tree. The strange stillness still hung heavy over the clearing, and left Eleri feeling uncertain.

Originally, Eleri had come to this clearing as a sort of pilgrimage. It was a remnant of an older, simpler time, before the magic faded. The air here was still charged with a natural power, like the legends said the world used to be, and many came just to bask in what was lost. Some came to use the inherent magic of the area to boost their own abilities, using it to complete spells that humans no longer had the native power to perform.

In days gone by, this clearing would never have stood out against the backdrop of magic that pervaded through the whole of Albion. But as magic was consumed and destroyed, something about it gave the great tree more staying power than other regions, and soon word of it spread.

Eleri knew of no explanation regarding why magic clung to the clearing; nothing she had learnt at her mother's side or in her own research gave any definitive answer. There were some whispered rumours that the tree itself was a prison, and that the magic came from the wizard imprisoned within, not that Eleri believed it. What wizard could be powerful enough to fuel others' spells, even through a magical drought, and yet remained trapped within a tree?

Eleri's reference book, which she had put in her lap while she fixed her hair, held a whole section about this clearing. It had started as a recording of her own childhood visit, and then expanded to include everything Eleri had discovered and theorised about. Still humming quietly, Eleri flipped to that section, currently marked with a strip of leather embroidered with stars, the same colour and style of her pack.

It was, in fact, a leftover piece from the making of her bag, repurposed to avoid wasting the material she had splurged on. She felt it added something to the look of her notebook, which by this point had become very raggedy from the years of use. The pages were all soft and worn, and the edges discoloured from frequent use. Nevertheless, it was one of Eleri's most prized possessions.

Looking at what she had written about this clearing, it was evident that most of what was known was based on hearsay and gossip. There wasn't even an official date for when the strange qualities of the area were first noticed, which made identifying what caused them even more difficult. Investigators from centuries back suggested that the clearing had been originally under a spell to divert attention away from it, which had faded over time, allowing people access to its magic. More modern magic scholars suggested that it was on an intersection of ley lines, or the site of some long-forgotten ritual, and its power only seemed strange and great compared to the drained magic present in most other places.

As fascinating as Eleri found the history to be, at this moment she was looking for something—anything—to explain the sudden lack of noise and movement. Her notes spoke little about the atmospheric qualities of the clearing; it seemed that most people reported that being near the tree was an amplifier for magic, especially for love-based spells, rather than a place where the world felt lacking. It came with a warning, however, that while the spells could induce feelings and form bonds between people, the results always made the spelled party feel some sense of trapped dissatisfaction, even if they never identified that they were under a spell.

Eleri had no use for love spells. She was rarely moved by amorous feelings, and even the rare chaste crush never factored much into her life plans. The amplifying effects for a person's magic were of no concern either, as increased nothing was still nothing. Frustrated with the lack of definitive answers, Eleri got up and started to pace a circle around the perimeter of the tree. This triggered another odd realisation: just as when she had been traipsing through the woods, the branches of the great tree brushed the top of her head and face, but none of them snagged her hair or scratched her skin. Eleri had brushed off the lack of debris caught in her plait as a coincidence the first time, yet it was now undeniable that it was a feature of the tree itself.

The branches felt more like a gentle caress than the haphazard result of two beings trying to exist in the same space. There was no pain or discomfort, but rather a sense of fondness and familiarity, like the tree itself was reaching for her, knew her in some capacity. Although Eleri still didn't hold with the idea that there was a person trapped within, perhaps there *was* something sentient about its magic, and it remembered Eleri from when she was a child.

For the first time, Eleri felt that she understood what other people had meant when they spoke about relatives who came up at family gatherings asking, *don't you remember me? You used to be so small.* The feeling was fleeting, and she swiftly dismissed it. There was no one out there who would remember her so fondly. Not here, not anywhere.

With a heavy sigh, mostly trying to break the oppressive silence that still hung over the clearing, Eleri stepped away from the tree. As she moved further from the reach of its branches, more and more of them clung to her hair and clothes. The thoughts of the mythical wizard still plagued her mind, but Eleri did her best to ignore that it felt like the tree was trying to hold on to her.

Her first pass at looking at the rune circle around the tree had been cursory, merely checking that it was nothing that would be activated by her presence or cause her harm. Now, Eleri turned to one of the blank pages she'd left in the section of her notebook dedicated to the clearing. After a quick detour to her pack for something to write with, Eleri began copying the ritual circle onto her page, paying careful attention to each detail.

The circle itself had an outer and an inner ring, and most of the complex, intersecting lines occurred on the inside. In the space between the two circles there were fewer markings, but it was also where the marked and mossy rocks sat. Once Eleri had reproduced the circle in her book, she began comparing the runes to her reference pages, making detailed notes about each one.

As Eleri puttered about the circle, a sense of urgency grew in her. It was unrelated to her findings, a strange type of fertility spell that would never have caused the unnatural silence around her. It was also unrelated to that silence, which, although oppressive and without cause, had not changed since she had first noticed it. She paused for a minute where she stood, close to the tree trunk again to examine the full view of the circle, to look around. Nothing had changed, there was still no one else around—no animals and none of the usual little forest sounds.

Exasperated by the odd feeling, and more than a little put out that she couldn't identify the cause of the vacuum-like silence, Eleri strode to the far end of the clearing and turned back to face it. She meant to get enough distance to take a proper look at the strange little forest opening, but what she saw took her breath away.

The tree's branches were reaching for her. Eleri couldn't write off her sense of unease as a strange feeling or a funny coincidence anymore. There was still no wind, but the whole of the great tree was bent towards her, every bough and twig straining to be closer to her.

Chapter Two

This almost life-like *reaching* was nothing like anything Eleri had ever seen. What strange manner of spell or enchantment caused the great tree to behave this way? Was it the same as the one that caused the eerie silence, or was it something else? For a moment, Eleri stood stock still, just watching the branches strain towards her. Perhaps it was in the vain hope that the nonexistent wind would die down and the branches would return to normal, or perhaps she just needed a moment to process what was in front of her.

The moment her wits returned, Eleri tossed her head back, straightened her shoulders, and marched back towards the tree, stopping only to pick up her pack along the way. She kept her hand on the hilt of her sword, though did not draw it yet. The second she was within reach, the branches enveloped her, folding around her as if to keep her from leaving again. It was an oddly affectionate gesture, filled with warmth, but it made Eleri's blood run cold. She had no frame of reference for what was happening now, not from her own life or from her studies.

The branches and her own curiosity ushered her forward. When Eleri reached the tree trunk again, the boughs gave a great shudder and the tree returned to normal. Its limbs no longer defied gravity to reach for Eleri. Instead, they hung inanimately, as if there had never been a force directing them to keep her close. Eleri put a hand on the trunk, closed her eyes, and did her best to *sense* what she could from the tree. Her mother, a witch of considerable power for this day and age, had more than once demonstrated a spell that would reveal any enchantments nearby. Eleri was incapable of such a feat, but she liked to think that with quiet contemplation of the world around her, she could gather some kind of knowledge.

The only thing Eleri felt was a feeling of impatient worry—her own, most likely.

Annoyed, she all but collapsed into the little hollow of the trunk again. She still had her notebook on her, so she took a moment to record what had just happened on another fresh page. From the dead silence of her surroundings to the uncanny behaviour of the great tree, Eleri made sure to write it all down as accurately as possible. She also included little asides to herself, about what she had already tried to uncover the reasons why, possible avenues of future research, and other little thoughts about her experience.

Despite writing it all down, nothing made sense to Eleri. Putting her thoughts on paper usually helped her work through her problems, or at least allow her to stop obsessing over them. She took a deep breath and exhaled it slowly through her nose, trying to purge herself of her frustration. It did not help.

With her legs curled up to fit in the tree's hollow and her notebook perched on her knees, Eleri felt rather *contained* by the tree, though the branches no longer reached for her, and she had put herself there by her own choice. It no longer felt like a refuge, and Eleri's mind strayed once again to the story of the trapped wizard. Eleri dropped her head to rest against the pages of her notebook.

"Frustrations upon frustrations," she muttered to herself.

With an air of annoyance, Eleri straightened somewhat and took to flipping through her book at random. It was her hope that this course of action would result in her seeing *something* that would give her a flash of inspiration about what was happening.

Perhaps another person could have chalked it up to one big mystery and moved on, but Eleri could not. She couldn't help but be absolute in her quest for answers. There had been times in the past when she had become so absorbed in her own research that it had consumed her for days, weeks, or even months at a time, pushing the thought of all other interests out of Eleri's head.

When nothing caught her eye, Eleri closed her notebook with a slow, deliberate movement. She grabbed her pack and jammed the book back into it. For a moment, she contemplated drop-kicking the bag across the clearing, but it did contain most of her worldly possessions, and was itself a not inexpensive purchase. Instead, Eleri set it down gently. She then pressed the palms of her hands against her eyes. It did not help with her agitation but did help soothe her burgeoning headache.

"Right," Eleri said. "Right. This is strange, but it's not inexplicable."

In spite of Eleri's attempts to convince herself, the weight of this mystery pressed down on her. A part of her wanted to pace, but a greater part was worried that doing so would trigger the tree to reanimate. Without the ability to pace, a restless energy started to grow within her. Unsure what else to do with herself, Eleri went back to examining the tree, going over each inch in excruciating detail.

She felt a little foolish, but Eleri pressed one ear to the trunk and knocked. It sounded like a normal tree. She shook off her embarrassment and straightened. She stood with her hands on her hips and tried to think of anything else she could do. With no other ideas forthcoming, Eleri turned to her last resort.

In a little pouch attached to the outside of her pack sat three little baubles. They were similar in size to dice, but were irregularly shaped, with sharp, multifaceted surfaces. Each of them shimmered slightly, and they were all darkly coloured and swirled with a multitude of hues.

Eleri undid the fastenings and took one out. She rolled it between her fingers, staring at it contemplatively. These baubles were Eleri's most expensive possession; even her prized travel pack paled in comparison to the cost of even one of the little things.

They were small bits of crystallized magic, *grym grisialau*, known colloquially as 'gryms.' Some mage, probably one who had dedicated their life to perfecting the creation of the fiddly little bauble, had spent days or even weeks building up their magical energy and coalescing it into something portable. Although rare, expensive, and good for only one use, it was perfect for any mage who needed a boost for their own powers, or a non-magic user like Eleri who needed minor magical intervention.

Some were weak, all-purpose magic, which were less expensive but also less reliable. Eleri tended to buy more specialised gryms, ones that sought to reveal secrets. It helped when she was out researching old magic sites, many of which had aspects to them that were lost to time along with the magic that had created them.

There was never enough power in the gryms to fully reveal the answers she sought, instead providing some kind of clue. Sometimes the magic would flip the pages of Eleri's notebook to a specific page, or it would cause a previously overlooked rune to glow briefly. Nevertheless, having a little hint when stuck in her research was invaluable. It was sometimes the difference between a breakthrough and hitting a metaphorical wall.

Still. The gryms were expensive. Eleri used them sparingly, only when she could find no other avenue forward. Like in this moment, where her frustration and confusion with the great tree and the atmosphere of the clearing was greater than any sense of frugality.

Eleri raised her left hand, one grym held tightly in her fist. She focused her thoughts on her questions about the clearing and squeezed the bauble.

Nothing happened.

Eleri lowered her hand and peeked inside her fist. The grym was still there, and it was intact. Eleri raised her hand again and did her utmost to concentrate only on activating the dormant magic within the crystal. Again, nothing happened.

Eleri gave a frustrated toss of her head, her long dark plait swinging aggressively. For a moment, she wondered if there was something wrong with the grym, or that she had been scammed and there was never any magic within it at all. Then, Eleri had a flash of realisation. It was possible she could use the remnants of enchantments left behind by magic users.

She put her hands on her hips and stared at the ground. With all the studying she had done of the rune circle, it was easy for her to locate the exact part she was looking for.

With a surreptitious glance at the great tree, Eleri carefully picked her way over towards the rune for magic amplification still burnt into the ground. Once she had her feet firmly planted, Eleri once again raised her hand.

"Lucky number three," she whispered to herself, hoping the rune circle and the grym would be able to work together despite there being no magic in her body to amplify their powers.

Eleri closed her eyes and took a deep, centering breath. When she opened them, she directed her thoughts only towards the mystery of the strange emptiness surrounding her, and squeezed the grym.

For the briefest of seconds, it seemed like there would be no reaction, like the first two attempts. Suddenly, the grym in Eleri's hand dropped in temperature. It was like holding an ice cube.

It was so cold that Eleri's first instinct was to drop it, but she set her jaw and held tight. At her feet, a sensation similar to dragging socked feet across a staticky carpet started to build. It made her toes curl in her boots. It was unlike any experience with any grym she'd ever had before.

Eleri held the frigid bauble aloft for another minute or two. Just as she was about to uncurl her fingers to examine it, the grym melted. More accurately, it liquified instantly, leaving a warm purple liquid to run down Eleri's wrist and into the sleeve of her blue tunic. Eleri brought her still closed hand closer to her face. Aside from the slight widening of her eyes when the bauble first melted, she wore no expression.

Eleri first turned her hand every which way, looking at the strange liquid. Finally, she opened her hand, palm up, to examine the remains of the grym. A very small amount of the swirly purple fluid remained in her palm, and she had to be careful to not accidentally spill it. It shimmered exactly like the grym had, but this was a reaction Eleri had never seen before.

The palms of Eleri's hand, and the parts of her fingers that had been in contact with the bauble, were tinged pink and were starting to tingle as they warmed up. She would have to keep an eye on it to make sure the cold hadn't done any long-term damage. There were no other marks on her skin. The gryms never left marks, but the reaction this time had been so strange that Eleri almost wished her hands had some evidence of it.

She dipped a finger on her other hand into the small puddle of the strange liquid. It was now lukewarm to the touch, slightly above the ambient temperature around her. Eleri brought that finger to her eye level and rubbed it against her thumb. The liquid had a strange slippery texture and smelled vaguely of burnt grapefruit. It was pungent enough to make Eleri wrinkle her nose in distaste.

Although the grym had started out as crystallised magic, the remnant fluid seemed as mundane as possible. What was left was likely just the oils, scents, and pigments the mage had used to personalise their gryms for the consumers. Like the clearing she stood in, it appeared that some force had completely removed or absorbed the magic. All that was left was the shell—completely inert.

Eleri quickly wiped her hands on her grey leggings. If her intuition was right, there was nothing in the purple liquid that could harm her. That didn't make her feel any more at ease, however, and she hurriedly flipped through her notebook one more time. Eleri jotted down her experiences with the grym, then jammed the notebook back into her pack.

With practiced movements, she donned her pack, attaching it to her belt so that it rested on her lower back beside her scabbard. Eleri then took one last look around the clearing, nodded to herself, and took off back the way she had originally come.

Unlike the carefree meandering that had brought her to the clearing, Eleri now sped through the woods. Her steps were both fleet and sure, and she paid no heed to the branches whipping at her face and body.

As Eleri got further and further from the clearing, the oppressive silence relented. Unfortunately, the strange, empty, dead quality of the atmosphere around her persisted, which only spurred Eleri on. Such a widespread and devastating change in the quality of the ambient magic had never happened in such a short time frame; not even the Great Corruption had been so rapid.

It was clear that there was something terrible going on with the magic in this area. Or, rather, there was something *removing* the magic from the area. Eleri had never seen anything absorb magic straight out of the gryms, but she was sure that was what happened. There was a force—Eleri did not know if it was natural, or the result of some spell or enchantment—that pulled the magic from the very atmosphere, and any magic introduced was immediately siphoned away as well.

This realisation, on top of the unsettling experience Eleri had just had with the semi-sentient tree branches, mostly unnerved Eleri. Even so, a small part of her couldn't help but be thrilled by the prospect of an adventure.

Chapter Three

The sun had just begun to dip below the horizon line when Eleri made it back to the little village where she was staying. Few people lived there, but it was the closest settlement to the magic pilgrimage site, so there was a decently-sized inn. The inn was obviously past its heyday, but there were still enough visitors to keep it worthwhile. Besides, the locals were fond of it as a tavern and catch-all meeting spot. Some used it as a wedding or other party venue.

The old man tending the service counter-cum-bar gave Eleri a strange look when she burst through the doors, but she paid it no mind. She knew she likely looked a little wild by that point. Her freckled nose and cheeks were pinked with exertion, a few locks of brown hair had been pulled free of her plait and hung loose besides her face, and she was panting slightly. The more Eleri had thought about the present situation, the more anxious she had become about starting to research. Finally unable to stand it any longer, she had run the last leg of the journey back to the inn, uncaring of the branches whipping at her legs, arms, and face.

Eleri took a deep breath to centre herself and wiped at her face—unknowingly smearing a streak of dirt across her right cheek. She then dusted off her leggings and made her way to the bar. With a bright smile that hid all her anxieties, she made quick work of ordering a bowl of the house stew. When she knew it was coming up, Eleri briefly excused herself to dash upstairs to her room, where she did a quick wash and twisted her failing plait into a low bun. Moderately refreshed, she returned to the inn's bar just as the innkeeper was putting her bowl of stew on the counter.

She did her best to savour each bite; it was quite good, but growing up with her mother had taught Eleri to never give her food enough time to grow cold. Soon enough, she was finished and back upstairs in her room. The first order of business for Eleri was to lay out her maps of Albion and the local area. She also dug through her pack to retrieve her notebook. Eleri took a moment to mourn the bent pages—the result of her hurried packing at the clearing, and the end of a years-long streak at keeping her book as neat as possible through the utmost care.

With her maps and research spread out on the floor, Eleri was able to begin her planning. The best thing to do, she thought, would be to start out by asking the locals if they had noticed anything suspicious lately. Then she would be able to take their insight and use it to plan her next move.

Eleri knelt on the floor next to her papers. She still had too much nervous energy to be satisfied with that simple plan, so she took to poring over her maps. With her left hand, she traced over the names of towns and landmarks, mentally mapping out the distances between and the best routes. At the same time, Eleri used her right hand to jot down two lists in her notebook—one of settlements she knew of with libraries she could use, and one of known magic sites.

Eleri sat back on her heels and twisted her ring absently. A sense of foreboding settled deep into her bones. The feelings of inadequacy her mother had worked so hard to instill grew and overwhelmed Eleri. If what she thought was true, that the last dregs of magic that had so strongly held on after the Great Corruption were disappearing, what could Eleri do? She had no magic of her own, and was an unnecessary and unwanted addition to her family line from birth. And yet, would it not be worse to turn her back on such a problem?

With that cheerful thought as her lullaby, Eleri reluctantly crawled into her cot and slept fitfully.

If the innkeeper last night had thought Eleri looked wild, he was to be proven right the next morning when he heard her questions. The excited flush had long since left her face, replaced with shadows under her eyes. Eleri was not an unfamiliar face in these parts, but she was usually a little more put-together and kept to herself—unless on an errand.

Her hip-length brown hair was loose today, its soft waves tamed only by the same twin blue ribbons holding it back from her face. This, paired with her doe eyes and the full apple of her cheeks, usually gave Eleri a disarming look, endearing her to others. Today, her exhaustion and worry were palpable, and she fidgeted with her ring incessantly, which, along with her strange questions about magic, was off-putting, to say the least.

"You haven't noticed anything unusual about the magic in the area? Not a strange feeling, or a lack of response when you try to use it?" Eleri asked the women gathered at the river, doing their washing.

"We don't have any mages here, girlie. Only those who come and go, visiting that big tree you went to see, and they don't talk much to us."

The woman who spoke was one of the oldest, and she seemed to have elected herself speaker of the group. It did not escape Eleri's notice either that the woman had positioned herself between her peers and Eleri.

"Think they're so special, don't they, Margie? Acting like they alone can save the world, but barely doin' a hard day's work anymore. Never got time for the little people, either," said another woman, middle-aged, with a small baby wrapped in cloth and secured tightly to her chest. She gave Eleri a hard look before dipping her chin to give the babe an absent-minded kiss on the head.

The old woman—Margie?—gave the young mother a dirty look, but ultimately sighed in agreement.

"Look, it isn't that we're ungrateful for you mages, you know, when the magic works. But so few of you come 'round here actually wanting to help us living here, instead of just looking at that thrice-damned tree and going home."

There were a few soft mumbles of agreement, and some of the washer women began drifting away from Eleri. Even Margie started to make the motions of packing up and moving on. "And then you all come around askin' us *questions* about the magic, as if we'd have any better idea about it just because we live here."

"Oh, I'm no mage!" Eleri clasped her hands behind her back and rocked back onto her heels. The renewed interest the washer women showed her was almost enough to soothe the familiar sting that phrase brought. "My mama was, though. She brought me here when I was little, and since she's... well, she's not with me anymore, I came back trying to find a way to connect with her."

The young mother's expression softened again, and her one hand came up to rest on her baby's back. Eleri fought the urge to crinkle her nose; she certainly had no desire to *connect* with her mother, the distance between them was a hard won one.

"Oh, your *mother*," Margie cooed. Eleri heard one of the older women mutter to a friend, *Ain't right for a little thing like that to not have a mother.* Eleri made sure her grin was firmly fixed on her face and apologised for the strange questions. It made her feel a little dirty to play on the women's sympathies like that, but she'd long since learned the art of putting people at ease when they found her unsettling or strange.

"I meant no disrespect. I was just hoping that someone here would know more about the great tree, and why it was so important to my mama," explained Eleri as she sat down on the shore to tug her boots and socks off.

Again, she was rewarded with odd looks from the washer women. She then rolled up her leggings and stepped into the water. With a more genuine, gentle smile, she held her arms open in a gesture of companionship.

"Please. I took up enough of your time today; let me help you get back on schedule."

Thus, Eleri finished her investigation of the small village, as unfruitful as it was, by splashing around good-naturedly and washing clothes in the river.

Eleri spent that night sleeping on the mossy ground of the forest. It was not the first time she'd done it, nor was it an unexpected turn of events. The distance between the little village Eleri had been staying at and the next town over with a library could be travelled on foot in a day, barely.

If Eleri had left that morning, as soon as she realised the locals had no idea what was happening to the magic right under their noses, it would have been doable. Helping the village women with their washing had certainly meant she'd have to take a pause in the forest, but Eleri couldn't feel any regret. Even with the rather sharp rock poking into her side.

Eleri rolled onto her back. She rarely slept in this position, usually curling up as small as possible, but the chance to lie back and see the stars was not one she could pass up.

Absentmindedly, Eleri reached one hand under her torso and swept the annoying rock away. Then she relaxed into the dirt, staring up at the little lights suspended in the night sky. With practiced ease, Eleri found the constellations of her childhood: the Hunter, the Dragon, the Queen, and the Bear.

Although she knew the constellation and the stories it inspired existed long before she did, Eleri drew cold comfort from the year-long presence of the Bear in the sky. As a child, she had imagined it to be her father, watching over her. Eleri had long abandoned this belief, but still enjoyed seeing it there, unchanging from night to night. From the Great Bear, she turned her gaze towards the Little Bear and the Northern Star.

When the sky was as dark as it was that night, it was possible for Eleri to understand how some could call the asterism a 'trail of fire'. She preferred the idea of a bear and its cub, though. When Eleri chose to examine those thoughts, she was forced to concede they were leftover from her childhood beliefs about her father—

and the idea that perhaps, somewhere, there was a parent who did not despair at the idea of their child following after them.

These maudlin thoughts annoyed Eleri. The weight of her discovery of the disappearing magic and self-appointed task to investigate it crushed her and brought her back to her lowest points, even as she tried to rationalise to herself that she had no definitive proof of any magical catastrophe yet.

Eleri folded her hands on her midsection and focused on the stars. After one more brief, longing glance at the Great Bear, Eleri sought out other constellations and asterisms. She silently recounted their stories to herself until sleep finally took hold of her.

The next day began early, with crisp, clear skies and a light breeze. Eleri was already on the move before the sun had fully risen. Her breath misted slightly in the dark morning air. This autumn had been quite warm, but without the sun the temperatures dropped at night regardless. Eleri repacked her belongings and, with one last look towards the still faintly visible North Star to ensure her orientation, set off.

Eleri mostly travelled in the dim light of dawn. By the time she crested the last hill before the next town, the sun was coming into its own, casting strong rays of light across the land. She still had roughly half an hour left to walk, but now Eleri would be able to travel in plain daylight.

This town was big enough that Eleri would have her choice between two inns. Although the town was still not very large, relatively, an old scholar had once retired there and had left her extensive collection of books—and her house to store them all—to the town. Locals and visitors alike were welcome to come peruse the books, provided they made a small donation and cleaned up after themselves.

Eleri chose the inn that was further away from the library. It was less expensive, and it meant she wouldn't have to spend her evenings with the same people she'd spent all day with, between the shelves. Besides, Eleri liked having time to walk and think after a hard day's work. She paid for a room but left nothing inside it. She had few belongings on her, and it seemed unnecessary to her to take a handful out just to bring the majority with her.

On her way through the town, Eleri stopped in at the bakery. There she purchased a loaf of fresh bread and two honey crispels. She ate the crispels outside the bakery while they were still warm, then continued on her way. She also stopped to buy a small wheel of cheese. This she kept wrapped up, intending to save it for her lunch. Her last stop was by the town's well, where Eleri took a moment to drink and clean the honey thoroughly from her hands. There were few patrons in the library when Eleri arrived, as she had expected. As she was staying in the far inn, she didn't know how many other travellers were in town to take advantage of the collection. Nevertheless, Eleri made sure she got there as early as possible, wanting to be slightly rude and commandeer an entire table for her research. She justified it to herself with the thought that there was the genuine possibility that she had uncovered a problem of massive proportions.

The table she selected was furthest from the door, partially hidden behind a large bookshelf. It wasn't the largest table available, which also soothed Eleri's misgivings about keeping it all for herself. Eleri spread her maps out on the table, then pulled out her notebook. On a spare bit of paper, she jotted down some beginning ideas to look up. These consisted mostly of the runes of the circle at the tree, to make sure the strange events weren't tied to that, and some on the history of the Great Corruption.

After flitting about between the shelves, Eleri amassed a good stack of books. Satisfied that she had enough material to begin her research, she returned to her seat. Eleri cracked open the first tome on her agenda, revelling in the scent of old books, and got down to business.

Chapter Four

Eleri straightened the books on the table, making the bottom corner of their spines all align perfectly. She let out a little huff of annoyance, partly because the books were all different shapes, which ruined the symmetry, but mostly at the lack of progress she was making. Mostly. The persnickety organisation of her supplies was more an extension of her frustration than an actual cause, but it was nice to have something tangible to fuss with.

There was little here Eleri didn't already know. It was clear the old eccentric was obsessed with the Great Corruption—likely living at a time when it was still believed that there was an easy fix—and her old collection reflected that. Eleri dutifully read through these books, looking for some scrap of information that may explain the strange acceleration she'd felt.

Eleri had known the basics of what caused the Great Corruption—everyone did. It was hard not to, when it affected every aspect of life. Her own personal interest in magic focused on the magic that remained, and the remnants of the time before, so Eleri had never delved so deep into the specifics of this era. Seeing the facts laid out in front of her in cold unfeeling text, made Eleri feel a little ill.

> The Great Corruption is a term used for the period in which there was an increase of 'corrupt' mages, specifically due to the cannibalistic ritual of heart-eating. By consuming the heart of another mage, one was able to 'absorb' their power. This was done by magically removing and eating the still beating heart while the victim was alive.
>
> The term, coined by Richard Dollawitz, has also colloquially been used to refer to recent years, when the number of mages being born and trained has decreased, and mages find it increasingly difficult to interact with ambient magic. Although it is generally accepted that this

> is a direct consequence of the Great Corruption, this author argues that it is an inaccurate use of the term. Without the clear distinction between the Great Corruption and its effects, it will become more difficult for research to focus on the discovery of a reversal.

Cannibal heart-eating. That was...new. Eleri slumped back against her chair and ran her hands down her face. She'd known the Great Corruption had been a result of mages stealing other mages' magic, and that the magic displaced from its true host had turned on its captor. People had whispered tales of corrupt mages growing more powerful and more distorted as they siphoned more and more magic in a bid to stay one step ahead of their own destruction. The cannibalism bit was usually left out. Eleri wondered if it had never been common knowledge, or if people had intentionally forgotten to soothe themselves as society continued to rely on magic to function.

> First proposed by Hathaway & James, the theory that the magic consumed by corrupt mages can no longer be reborn into the world—either through new mages or by returning to the ambient magic—is generally accepted by the community at large. Knowles, in his seminal paper on nature magic and spirituality, suggested that corrupt magic could be re-consumed and purified. Although largely debunked, the other aspects of his theory, namely the process in which corruption occurs....

Eleri put the book down, allowing the sentence she'd been reading to trail off in her mind. Her own grandfather had suffered from corruption. Eleri didn't know it was possible for her to despise him more than she already had, but that was before she knew he had eaten at least one human heart. On top of the disgust she felt for that action, Eleri also felt a flash of hot, selfish anger.

If her grandfather hadn't stolen magic, hoarded it in his own body, would Eleri have been born with magic? Instead of being the first in a long line of mages without it? Would that simple change have been enough to make her mother—? But no. Aside from the fact that that line of thinking was short-sighted when faced with the greater consequences of the Great Corruption, thinking about Eleri's mother was guaranteed to bring only pain.

Reading the rest of the books on the Great Corruption only told Eleri more of the same information. It was clear that little further research beyond that point had been conducted. Not even the patrons of this little library seemed interested, as the books Eleri found were covered in a thick coating of dust.

Based on the records the library kept, it seemed that most people came here to look for solutions to their personal magical problems—either the specific spell, or some fanciful remedy to give or bolster magical power.

Eleri blew a loose strand of hair out of her face. Aside from a depressing revelation about her own family, she'd uncovered nothing in her research. Had this been a regular project, one of her own little passions, Eleri would have been mildly put out at this turn of events. Research wasn't always as linear or easy as one might like. This, however, felt too important to let fester over months.

Truly, she had no real evidence for her theory; the strange happenings at the great tree's clearing could be a result of the magic in that area, not the Great Corruption, even if it felt like a loss of magic more than an effect of the same. Eleri leaned back in her chair, right thumb gently rotating the ring on her adjacent index finger. A part of her balked at taking her time with this problem, an unusual feeling that rebelled against her usual meticulous nature, which liked to consider a problem from every angle. To stave off the growing dread, Eleri took to rearranging her books again.

I'm just agitated because of what Grandfather did, she told herself, stacking and restacking her entire fodder of books. That one was too narrow to be on the bottom, but *this* one was too short.

There's no reason to worry just because a little bit of magic didn't work for you, that's hardly unusual, is it?

"Hey, you."

The harsh but not unfriendly voice broke through Eleri's concentration. It was an older man, long beard more grey than anything else. He was familiar, but not one of the townspeople Eleri knew. The man gestured at one of the books on spells she hadn't got to yet.

"Mind letting us see that book for a sec? Ol' Tom's having a spot of trouble and needs it."

Eleri gave a small nod and slid the book towards him. The man grabbed it and—didn't run, but certainly left faster than he usually walked. Curious, and more than a little tired of her research, Eleri followed him. She wasn't the only one, either. Other visitors followed the man out of the library, and there was a crowd of locals mingling anxiously waiting for him outside. The strange collection of people followed the man through the town to a little house by the outskirts of the town with a large field behind it.

Next to the small house stood the family, and the town's only mage. Tom, though younger than the bearded man who had come to fetch the book, was more wrinkled and tired-looking than him. His blond hair was shot through with premature grey and looked as washed out as the wheat field he and the farmer were surveying. The sun beat down on them all, dry and hot, and even Eleri's untrained eye could see that the harvest was to be poor that year.

There was already a crowd milling about, whispering anxiously among themselves, and vying for a better position. It was not uncommon for people to gather to watch mages work, but there was a tension in the air that was unusual. Rather than join the throngs of people, Eleri hoisted herself up to sit on the sturdiest-looking fence post, from which she had a decent enough view.

The older man from the library had to push his way through to the door. Eleri could hear some grunts and exclamations, until the man shouted:

"Out of the way! I've got the damn book!"

When he was finally in front of the house, the man gave the book to the mage, who accepted it grimly. There was a moment where Tom flipped through the book before he settled on a page and turned towards the wheat field again. Eleri knew that book was one on the relationship between magic and plants—she'd chosen it thinking mostly of the strange old oak tree—and a small thrill went through her at the thought she may see a mage renew a whole crop. There were few left with that kind of power.

Tom wrapped a chain with a small pendant—his conduit, Eleri surmised, the personal item that allowed modern mages access to the magic around them—around his hand and knelt, pressing his closed fist against the dry dirt. He looked at the page in the book and read the spell.

Nothing happened. The mage tried again, with a more forceful pronunciation. Someone in the crowd shouted out the suggestion that the mage use some form of amplifier, and there was a shuffle in the crowd as people tried to be the one to hand theirs to him. Finally, the group got itself organised enough to pass both a paper with an amplifying spell and a grym to Tom.

Tom, who had flipped through the library book helplessly a few times, took both items as they were handed to him. He wiped the accumulated sweat from his brow and got back into position. He wrapped the amplifier paper around the grym and held it in his left hand, then raised the grym in a familiar gesture. Again, Tom read the spell, this time in a near shout.

Immediately, the mage shouted again and shook out his fist. Splashes of fluid and pieces of half-liquefied magic were flung about, drawing shocked exclamations from the inhabitants. Almost concurrently, a shout rang out from the crowd of witnesses:

"Fire! There's a fire!"

There was a scramble, which ended when one of the family's children dumped the washbasin of clothes left by the drying line on the small flame. Without the active flame, it was easy to see that the fire had been the result of the paper amplifier burning, curling in on itself as it self-destructed, and igniting the dry grass.

Eleri's heart was in her throat. Around her, people began whispering among themselves. The noise was simultaneously too loud and still felt like she was hearing it from several rooms away.

"Ol' Tom's never failed like that before..."

"D'you think he's lost his touch?"

"Gods, what are we gonna do? Lucy in the next village over can't do potions anymore either."

"Heard about that! They're just foul-tasting drinks now, aren't they?"

"It's not just us, you know! The cloth merchant who came by yesterday told me it's the same in the next three towns, too!"

The farmer and Tom drifted off to the side, discussing something quickly and quietly. Others, whom Eleri recognised as the rest of the local farmers, came to join them. It did not look like a happy conversation, and finally it ended with a firm shake of Tom's head. The grim-looking mage walked off quickly, so as to deter other conversations, but with an unmistakable air of defeat.

Eleri slid off the fence post. Even though her mind was a million miles away, she still dismounted with a practiced ease. She was already on her way back to the library when the farmer regained his bearings enough to shoo the gathered people away from his house.

Still in a half daze, Eleri sat back down at her claimed table. All the books still stacked there now seemed both meaningless and incredibly daunting. At least it was now confirmed that the events at the great tree were not localised to that area, or because Eleri herself was not a mage. The last dregs of a magic that had persisted for so long were now finally dying out.

Eleri shuffled her stack of books aimlessly. She knew what all of them contained, but the enormity of the problem made it difficult for her to find the motivation to start. Slumped in her seat, Eleri fiddled with her rings, deep in thought. It would be possible to continue as she had been, slowly working her way through stacks upon stacks of books, bouncing from library to archive to records hall and gleaning small bits of information at a time, trying to synthesize them into something useful, something that would explain this new dearth of magic. Possible, but time-consuming. Maybe more so than anyone had time for.

The other option—and here Eleri bit her lip, deep in thought, then pressed the ring of her right index finger to her lips—the other option was to find an expert.

Eleri was not normally one to shy away from her own inadequacies. If she didn't know something, she wanted to learn. If she wasn't good at something, she wanted to practice. Her own inability to do magic was the only exception; even after years of studying the history and theory behind it, trying every possible conduit, there was not a single spell she could cast. There was always a sense that Eleri *did* understand magic in the innate way only mages were supposed to, at least according to her, but that did not translate to practical skill. It seemed to her that what she knew about herself was at odds with the reality she lived in. Even now, having had years to get used to it, her lack of magic brought Eleri's mood down when she thought of it.

Eleri used her notes to cross-reference the contents of the books. It was a mostly empty gesture; she knew she had absorbed all possible information from these books, but it was nice to be thorough. It was also nice to put off the next step.

When Eleri could not deny it any longer, she packed up all her supplies. Her notes and maps were carefully folded and returned to their usual place in her pack. Then she returned all the books she had been studying from, placing them neatly on the stack of returns a volunteer was responsible for shelving every night.

Next, Eleri left the library. She turned away from the inn she'd been staying at, unsure if she wanted to spend one more night or move on immediately. Instead, Eleri went towards the town hall. The doors were barred, and a group passing by told her that all the members of the town's council were gathered to discuss the events of the afternoon.

That was of no consequence to Eleri. She had already come to her own conclusions about what she had seen and would be soon getting a second opinion from a more learned source. Hopefully.

On the message board that stood just outside the town hall, Eleri found what she was looking for. There, in a neat, printed page—the same kind that had been seen in every village every year since the Great Corruption—was a list of days and correlating villages. It was the list of all upcoming Trials in the area. Eleri jotted the ones happening the soonest down, then returned to the inn, deciding to rest for one more night.

Chapter Five

The crowds of people pressed against Eleri from all sides, suffocating to the point where she almost relented and fled. Almost.

Although it was already late autumn, the drought and dry heat were worse in this region, which was further south than she had been in a while. This contributed to Eleri's discomfort, being one who did not tolerate the heat well. Eleri had opted to wear just her blue tunic and grey leggings, long brown hair tamed into a plait that hung down her back to her hips. Even pulled back and tamed, the weight and presence of her hair made sweat gather at the base of Eleri's neck. Her black cloak, usually a staple for this time of year, had been left at her little campsite just outside of town. Eleri knew better than to expect there to be space at the inn. The village of Oldawynn was not built to support this many people, just large enough to warrant having its name on a map. Those living in smaller towns and in rural areas flocked there every year for the council visit, even those not taking part in the Trials. It was a good time to see old friends, buy new things, and, of course, take note of any new magic users. Eleri made a habit of avoiding the Trials wherever and whenever they happened, but when an expert mage was needed and no other option available, she resigned herself and did her best to stay on the fringes of the festivities.

The crowd swept Eleri towards the town centre, where the same rickety old stage was erected every year. Three figures in hooded purple robes presided over the entire affair.

Just the sight of the pomp and circumstance made Eleri burn with a mix of anger, humiliation, and jealousy. A distant part of her noted that the reaction was as strong as it had been when she was a child, despite the years in between.

At that moment, a young boy with an unruly mop of red hair was being led across the stage. His face and body language made it clear he was nervous, and the ravenous stares of the assembled people didn't help. One of the hooded figures kept a firm grip on the boy's shoulder, which Eleri assumed was to prevent him from bolting.

At centre stage there was a table with several items on it. Each item was chained to the table with thick iron, scrolling symbols in an ancient language etched into each link. Some of the items Eleri could see were a staff, a wand, a cauldron of something bubbling, and a small pendant. They represented all the possible ways for mages to channel their limited power the conduits for forcing it out into the world.

The little boy, now sniffling softly, was directed to touch each item in turn, to no avail. He'd made it through almost the whole selection with nothing to show for it, until the cauldron. The boy was so small he had to strain his arm and rise to the tips of his toes just to reach the handle of the spoon, but the second his fingers curled around the handle of the utensil, violet sparks erupted from the cauldron.

The boy had magic, then.

The crowd erupted in shouts and cheers, some congratulating the boy, some offering apprenticeships, and some already bargaining for work. Using potions as a conduit for magic was becoming less common, making this an even more auspicious outcome than usual.

Eleri grit her teeth. Unlike the townsfolk, she found the revelation of the boy's magic was nothing to cheer about. It served as a miserable reminder of her own experiences with the Trial, in addition to her normal gripes about magical conscription.

Gripped with the all-consuming urge to escape, Eleri began weaving her way through the throngs of people, desperate to at least find somewhere with space to breathe. The crowd was so thick, especially near the stage, that people seemed to be packed in, almost compressed to each other. The Trials were simply too important for anyone to miss.

Anyone thought to have even the slightest magical gift was forced to attend the Trials these days. Before the Great Corruption, mages were discovered naturally, either coming into their gifts on their own or being recognised by one of the local magic users. Or, in times long gone when the ambient magic was strong, some mages were not born with any natural gift, but could use magic through dedicated study. That hadn't happened in generations. As the number of mages declined suddenly and drastically—and their already diminished numbers continued to shrink every year—the people of Albion soon began conscription of all known mages into the efforts to preserve the existing magic.

They could be nominated by themselves, their family, or anyone who had reason to believe that magic lurked within their veins, personal thoughts on the matter be damned. Children, younger every year, were paraded in front of their peers to test their abilities; not only were most adults already tested, but it was believed that the younger the child was when discovered, the most use of their abilities could be garnered.

On the stage, the little red-haired boy continued to cry. He now sat with other children, presumably the other successful Trial candidates, where he sobbed despondently for his mother. A similar-looking woman stood on the edge of the stage, scolding the boy for his ingratitude in the face of such honour, ignoring the way he reached for her.

Eleri left town.

Distancing herself from the memories and the crowds was not going to help her, Eleri knew that. She'd have to get herself into the middle of the throng of people and catch the attention of one of the hooded figures. Even if they weren't a true member of the magic council, they were important enough to represent Gryphon's Keep and all the mages at the Trial. The Keep was the stronghold of magic. All the most learned mages congregated there to share their experiences, research, decide on the conventions of use, and, in recent years, regulate the Trials.

Of course, Eleri had no illusion that *important* necessarily meant *intelligent,* but she hoped that someone from Gryphon's Keep would have more information than the average person.

Eleri stretched out along the campfire she had built, half-reclining on one arm as she stared into the flames. If there was one good thing about her strategic retreat, it was that she now had time to consolidate her thoughts and plan her questions. There were more than a few members of the Keep who viewed themselves above non-magic folk and believed that they were given the gift of magic for a reason, which said something about the level of prestige they deserved. And no one was more worthless than someone who had failed the Trials, who had aspired to heights above their station and had to be brought back down to Earth.

Unable to help herself, Eleri rolled her eyes. Even just thinking about their attitude made her annoyed. She had been fiddling with a small stick but threw it into the fire. Then Eleri sat up and began rummaging through her pack. She spared a brief thought for how whatever she needed always seemed to be at the bottom of the bag, then managed to extract a small metal cup and a tin of tea. She also pulled out a tea strainer and her water skin.

Eleri filled the cup halfway full of water, then put it on a flat rock she'd put off to the side of the fire. When the water was boiling, Eleri wrapped her hand in a length of cloth, and removed the cup from the heat. Even with her hand protected, it was almost painfully hot. She filled the cup the rest of the way, bringing the water down to a more manageable temperature. Then she filled the strainer and left the tea to steep. It wasn't the most practical way to make tea, and it did change the flavour somewhat, but Eleri knew how to make do. The last thing to do was add a spoonful of honey—just a tiny dollop, as she was almost out.

The tea helped settle her mind. Eleri used this newfound peace to help ready herself for sleep. The day had been long, noisy, and filled with bad memories. Eleri banked her fire and got comfortable in her bedroll. She curled up as small as possible, watching the glow of the embers. Tomorrow would be the day that she got some answers about this mess.

The next morning brought with it a kind of drizzling half-rain. There was certainly precipitation falling, but not heavily enough for it to be of any real consequence. Even that was a blessing, though, after the near-drought conditions Albion had faced all summer and into the autumn. Eleri's hair was damp, the loose waves frizzing up, but it was not actually wet. Eleri ran her hands over her brown locks, trying to tame them where they lay over her shoulder. She kept up this almost meditative action as she walked back into town.

It was still very early in the morning, so Eleri had no trouble getting a table at the tavern for breakfast despite the increased population. This particular tavern was more expensive than she usually chose, but its price and proximity to the town centre made it the most likely place to run into one of the Elders of Gryphon's Keep. Eleri was just beginning her meal of eggs and toast when her plan came to fruition.

A pair of Elders entered the tavern, rich purple hoods pulled over their heads against the rain. Eleri had just been wondering how to approach them, as they were undoubtedly about to be swarmed by townsfolk, when they removed their hoods. At the sight, Eleri grimaced and ducked her head, debating on the merits of choosing another target for her questions.

It was a futile gesture. One of the Elders saw her and started coming towards her. He was an old man, still spry for his age, with white and grey hair and a craggy face. He waved his companion off, then took a seat opposite Eleri. He smiled vacantly at her, obviously waiting for a greeting.

Eleri ignored him, taking another bite and resolutely looking away from the ghost from her past.

"It's very rude to ignore an old friend, little Ellie," he said, his voice full of patronising rebuke.

"My name isn't Ellie," she told him simply, then added, "If we were truly friends, you'd know that."

The man's smile slipped for a second, then was back in full force. He chuckled like Eleri had told a joke, but it was forced.

"Friend of your mother, then. And I can't help it, I've known you since you were a little girl!" He reached forwards to pat her hand.

Any friend of my mother is no friend of mine, Eleri thought sourly. She pulled her hand back and tucked it in her lap along with the other one.

"Is there anything I can do for you, Master Dewi? I'm certain you and your compatriot are positively *swamped* with work," Eleri asked.

They stared at each other for a moment, a battle of wills, then Eleri decided he wasn't worth a cold breakfast. She picked up her toast and angled it, so her next bite cut straight into the yolk. She preferred her eggs very runny and knew Dewi hated to see the yolks pool. He made a face when the first drop hit her plate, and Eleri grinned. It was well worth the unfortunate consequence of sticky hands to see that expression. Maybe Dewi would be so disgusted he would leave.

No such luck. Instead, Dewi gestured at his companion across the room, someone Eleri did not recognise, and the other figure went on to get a table of their own. It seemed Dewi was here to stay.

"Tell me, what news do you have of my old friends Simon and Megan?" Dewi asked with false casualness.

Eleri inclined her head towards her plate, unwilling to show Dewi the look of discomfort that was surely on her face at the mention of her mother and grandfather. She unfolded the napkin that had been in her lap and wiped her hands.

"None," Eleri said simply, then ignored the Elder in favour of her tea.

It was clear that Dewi was expecting her to offer a reply with more substance, and when she didn't, a brief look of annoyance flashed across his face. Or perhaps it was because of the silent treatment; he was not a man used to being ignored. He reached out again and took hold of her elbow from across the table.

"You aren't playing very nice, little Ellie," he said. "You ought to go home and learn some manners. I know your mother wouldn't want her only daughter behaving like this to someone like me."

Eleri twisted her arm and watched in satisfaction as the movement dragged Dewi's cuff through a puddle of yolk on her plate.

He made a noise of disgust and let go of her arm to rear back. As Dewi was dabbing at his sleeve with a handkerchief, Eleri caught his eye. She pointed at her plate.

"You put your arm in my food," she told him, her voice carefully neutral.

"I! You! Ugh!" Dewi floundered, then glared at Eleri. "You are as impossible to talk to as ever! It's lucky you failed the Trials; I would despair for whoever became your teacher otherwise!"

Then he shoved his chair away from the table and stormed off, muttering about how difficult it was to clean the fabric of his robes. Eleri watched him go, then turned her attention back to her breakfast. It was no longer very appealing, cold and soiled as it was. Still, Eleri picked at the last bits of toast.

"You shouldn't be so rude to an Elder," a male voice said from somewhere behind her, one of the other patrons, surely. "You don't understand the pressure they're under."

"What I don't understand is how a man could get to be that old and still act like a brat," Eleri retorted.

"The Elders are the last bastion of our way of life," the unknown man insisted. "Not that you'd know; I'm sure anything to do with magic is *far* beyond your grasp, even who to thank for it."

Eleri rolled her eyes. She stood, arranged her used dishes and utensils nicely, and made her way towards the door. As she passed the man, she paused briefly.

"I have nothing to thank the Elders for," Eleri said coolly. Then she left.

Chapter Six

Eleri drifted vaguely through the streets. The village of Oldawynn had long been a favourite of hers, filled with squat stone buildings topped with thatched roofs, all decorated with wood designs. Today there were signs of the festivities all around, from the banners and streamers hanging from every available surface to wreaths and garlands of flowers decorating buildings. There were plenty of little stalls set up, everywhere and anywhere the vendors could find space. Some were the village's usual wares, but vendors from all over the region had poured in to get their wares seen by a wider audience as well.

Eleri tried to lose herself in the atmosphere of excitement. There were only a few others out and about this morning, which made it easy for her to take a moment and look at all the stalls she passed. Although Eleri wasn't looking to make any purchases, it was nice to see what these folks were so passionate about.

The walking also helped Eleri calm her mind. By using some of her energy to move her body, it left less for her brain to use to overthink. It also worked off the last of the tension and annoyance brought on by the encounter with Dewi.

As the matter stood, there was honestly no real reason for Eleri to continue pursuing this mystery. Personally, yes, she liked to see things through to the end and preferred a definitive answer, but if Gryphon's Keep knew about the vanishing magic and was researching it, what more could Eleri offer? She wasn't going to be the one to break the news to the experts, and without magic, she was destined to be nothing more than an amateur researcher.

It would be pure arrogance to assume that she was the *only* one needed to solve this problem, but Eleri also couldn't stand the idea of walking away from an issue without trying to make it better. She knew rationally that her childhood had instilled a sense of inadequacy in her, but knowing that didn't make the incessant need to *fix* and *help* and *justify her existence* any less powerful.

Eleri's musings were cut short by the sensation of a small body all but crashing into her, accompanied by a gleeful shout. She caught a glimpse of a blonde head burying itself in her stomach as she was hugged, then Eleri's sight was distorted as more children swarmed her. They all spoke excitedly, their voices becoming an incomprehensible babble. They clustered in as close to Eleri as possible, hands grabbing at her own and her tunic as each vied for her attention.

"All right, all right!" Eleri laughed, gently guiding them away from her. "My! How tall you've all gotten!"

This set the children off again, but this time Eleri had the space to usher them out of the middle of the path. There was something about Eleri that drew children to her, and she had more patience for them than most adults. In the majority of the towns she visited, there was at least one child who eagerly looked forward to her next appearance. Not only did Eleri bring stories from far away, but also did her best to bring them sweets and little trinkets picked out individually for each child.

In Oldawynn, there were two sets of siblings among that group. The first, a pair of brothers, were quick to draw Eleri's attention. She'd known them since the younger was a baby, when Eleri had been the one responsible for fetching a rare herb for a healing tincture that had saved the infant's life. Their parents had ensured the boys knew and were grateful to Eleri for that, but it had turned into a much deeper relationship over the years. It had been one of the first jobs Eleri had done after she'd run away from home, and the couple had taken care of Eleri, young and sickly herself. Even now, Eleri was sure to spend at least a few hours with the boys when she passed through Oldawynn.

Once the boys had happily told Eleri of their recent accomplishments and been rewarded with a pocketful of treats, they cleared the way for others to do the same. The passel of children kept Eleri busy for a while but had mostly cleared by the time the last set of siblings became the center of attention.

The oldest, who had been the one to all but tackle Eleri initially, was a little girl who had clung to her waist the entire time. Her brother, barely more than a toddler, was also pressed close to Eleri. Young as they were, Eleri viewed the pair of them as dear friends, and was always delighted to see them. Like the others, they cheerfully informed Eleri of their recent escapades before being sent on their way with a treat. The sister dutifully led her brother off, but then they turned as one and rushed back for one last hug. Wrapped in their little arms, Eleri felt more at peace than she had since before visiting the great oak. She was hard-pressed to let them go, but eventually did. Then Eleri was alone again and took to wandering the town streets yet again.

Eventually, Eleri came to the town centre. The wooden stage was still standing, looking rickety and worn down now that it was empty. It took up most of one side of the square, stretching from corner to corner and coming almost to the very middle. People continued on around it, but now that it was empty, they gave it annoyed looks, as they had to detour around it. It was a far cry from the reverence they had shown it during the Trials.

Eleri made her way over to the stage. She swung herself up onto the platform, avoiding the stairs and the memories they would surely trigger, and sat herself on the edge. She was short, so Eleri's legs dangled, and she kicked them gently in the air. The town was starting to truly wake up, so her seat on the stage would soon become an excellent place to people-watch.

Eleri sat there for a while; she wasn't sure how long. Soon the streets were filled with people going about their day, and the sounds of children laughing and vendors self-promoting. Eleri watched all this, half-lost in thought and humming quietly to herself.

As the day progressed, the sun shone brighter. Just as Eleri was beginning to think she might like to go find something to drink, she caught sight of a young woman walking towards her quite purposefully. She was of medium height, with clear, dark skin, and looked to be a few years older than Eleri. As this was the first person to approach Eleri since she'd sat down, she decided to see how it played out.

"Hi!" said the woman as soon as she was close enough to be heard. "If you're looking to talk to the Elders, they won't be here until it's time for the next Trial, and someone is going to come clear the area before that."

"That's very kind of you to let me know, but I'm just here to people-watch," Eleri replied.

The excitement in the woman's eyes dimmed.

"Oh. I see." She then perked up again. "Are you one of the people going through the Trial this evening?"

"No." Once again, Eleri's response seemed to be a disappointment to this woman. "Are you hoping to find an apprentice or something at the Trials?"

The woman laughed and waved off Eleri's question.

"No! I've got barely enough training under my belt to be considered a full-fledged mage, I'm not ready to be responsible for someone else's education."

She hopped up onto the stage next to Eleri and stuck out her hand. Eleri shook it.

"My name's Sioned. Actually, I've been following the Elders around from place to place, hoping to get a chance to talk with one of them."

"Not the easiest of tasks," Eleri agreed. Before Eleri could say more, Sioned leaned around her and waved, the same sunshine bright smile on her face.

Turning to see who Sioned was waving at, Eleri could just catch a glimpse of a tall, icy blonde woman ducking her head awkwardly, then raising her hand in return.

"Sorry," Sioned said. "I've seen that woman around quite a lot recently, so I've decided to try being friendly."

Sioned and Eleri watched the tall blonde quickly duck into the nearest shop, almost catching her own hand in the door in her hurry to close it.

"I don't think she likes me much." Sioned shrugged. "Not that I'm having much luck with the Elders, either."

"Hm. What do you need to talk to the Elders for? Aren't they notoriously difficult to get in touch with?" Eleri knew the answer, but felt it was the appropriate question to ask.

Sioned sighed despondently. Her smile had dimmed when the blonde woman rebuffed her greeting, but now it fell off her face entirely.

"It's been my dream since forever to become an Elder myself. I know it's supposed to be a challenge to become one, they only want the best of the best, and I guess getting to talk to one is the first obstacle."

Eleri thought Sioned's explanation was bullshit but didn't say so. She was unsure of how much Sioned believed herself, and how much of it was her trying to convince herself to not give up.

The two young women sat quietly for a moment. Eleri was still thirsty, but Sioned's company was enjoyable even in silence. She exuded a kind of warmth and was so personable that her unprompted conversation had been pleasant, rather than strange to Eleri.

"I don't mean to be rude, but why don't you just visit Gryphon's Keep? Wouldn't that be easier than trying to catch the attention of an Elder when they're at their busiest?"

Eleri's question broke the silence, but it quickly returned and turned awkward as Sioned only stared at her in disbelief. Finally, Sioned shook her head and let out a strangled laugh.

"You must not have magic at all, do you—?" Sioned broke off, as she realised she hadn't learned Eleri's name. "Well, it's just that the location of the Keep is a closely-guarded secret, it's been hidden for years, and you only get to go there if you're invited."

"Even if you have reason to go, it's a nightmare trying to get an invitation," another voice cut it.

Both Eleri and Sioned whipped around to find the tall blonde from before standing there. She scratched at her face self consciously.

"Sorry. I just overheard your conversation as I passed by. I'm Clara, and I wish it was as simple as just going to Gryphon's Keep."

Sioned gave a delighted little laugh. She immediately reached for Clara's hand and grasped it with both of her own.

"I'm Sioned! I've seen you around Oldawynn, and I think even at the last town, too. You must also be trying to get in touch with an Elder."

Clara flushed lightly. The two of them kept talking, comparing stories of their futile attempts to get an invitation to Gryphon's Keep. Sioned was clearly thrilled to be given the opportunity to make friends with the blonde, while Clara still seemed rather reserved, and maybe a bit shy.

Eleri tuned them out. She was so far from being on the same page as the other women; not only was she not trying to get an invite to the Keep, she generally preferred to avoid both it and its inhabitants at all times. Only in few circumstances was she willing to consider travelling in that direction. However... it would be a means to an end, if she wanted to know the Elders' thoughts on the Great Corruption. When the conversation reached a natural lull, Eleri broke in.

"I can take you to Gryphon's Keep."

Again, Sioned looked at her strangely. "Pardon? Could you say that again?"

"I doubt that, how would you know the way? It's not like the Keep is even open to the public." Clara rolled her eyes.

"I suppose it once was," Eleri answered, spinning her ring again. "Back in the days when everything magic related was easier. I've been there many times and have guided others there before. From Oldawynn to Gryphon's Keep is just about a week's travel."

"You just... take people to the Keep?" Sioned asked, sounding strangled.

Eleri just nodded. Suddenly, Clara seized her by her shoulders. It was not a painful grip, but it was an intense one.

"And you'll take us there? Now?" Clara demanded.

Eleri nodded again. "We can leave today, if you'd like that."

Chapter Seven

Sioned had asked that they stay one more night in Oldawynn, and Clara had reluctantly agreed. The argument that it was hardly worth losing out on the money they'd already paid for another night at the inns they'd been staying at had won the blonde over.

For her part, Eleri had spent the extra time going over the supplies needed to bring three people to Gryphon's Keep. Most she had on hand, but there were a few things she decided to pick up in the morning before they left.

When it was all said and done, the trio of women did not set out on their journey until nearly noon. After seeing Eleri purchase supplies, both Sioned and Clara had wanted to do the same—especially Sioned, who had nothing suitable for sleeping outside. The first day they travelled together was uneventful. It consisted mostly of Sioned and Clara making small talk with Eleri sometimes joining in. As they walked further and further from Oldawynn, the festivities and noise decreased and shifted into the gentle sounds of nature. Eleri took to showing her companions the basics of how to track and forage for edible plants, and this made up the majority of her contributions to the conversation.

When it was nearing evening, Eleri, Clara, and Sioned came to a tiny village. Most of the villagers had made their way to Oldawynn for the Trials, but there were a handful of people still at home. They were mostly the old or infirm, those whose bodies were not equal to travelling all day. One such old lady allowed the three young women to stay the night in her house, in exchange for help darning clothes—the woman's eyes were no longer as good as they once had been.

Even though Eleri had worked late into the night, sewing by candlelight, the three women still left the village early in the morning. The dew was still fresh on the ground when their host saw them off, waving good-naturedly before going back inside her house. Clara and Sioned yawned periodically as they walked. They had also stayed up with Eleri but had done less of the actual darning. Both had tried their best but were clearly unpracticed. Sioned held the needle with some skill but could not patch the holes, and Clara was a novice at sewing completely. Their main contribution that night was company.

Sioned had talked animatedly the whole time, both with her fellow travellers and the old woman, but Clara had awkwardly avoided answering for the most part. The blonde had watched Sioned as she spoke, but swiftly ducked her head to focus on her needlework when Sioned turned to face her. Clara's face would also flush slightly when Sioned would rest her hand on her arm, or even just put her face too close to Clara's. Despite this, Clara had sat next to Sioned all night, even when Eleri offered to trade places.

Eleri was grateful for the quiet, sleepy morning. There was less conversation as they walked, as none of them felt particularly chatty that morning. Although Eleri had no problems with Sioned's talkative nature and had quite enjoyed listening to her at some points, she was pleased to have time to herself to think.

The first sounds they truly heard that morning, aside from farmers starting their day and birds chirping, was the sound of a pack of dogs barking. Eleri moved to the side of the road they were on, expecting a hunting party to pass them by, but there was no one else in sight. Anyone with a pack of dogs large enough to make that much noise should have been visible on the road, or at least as movement through the trees in the forest on either side of the women.

As the strangeness began to sink in for them, the three women grew tense. After a few moments looking up and down the road and not seeing the source of the noise, Eleri led them further into the woods. The sound of the barking grew louder and quieter seemingly at random; sometimes growing closer and others sounding further away. Still, the trees around them showed no signs of being disturbed by a hunt.

Eleri crouched down and examined the forest floor by gently moving fallen leaves aside. It took her a moment, but soon enough she stood again with a little noise of triumph. She called Clara and Sioned over.

"See these tracks?" Eleri pointed. There, in the soft dirt she had uncovered were the prints of cloven hooves. "See how they are pointed at the top? Like a deer, but these tracks are bigger, and the hooves have spread under the weight of the animal."

Sioned made appropriately interested noises as Eleri explained, but Clara watched the demonstration with a critical eye.

"So? There's a deer in the area? I could have guessed that from the sound of the hunting dogs." Clara scoffed.

Eleri grinned widely. It showed off a sharp and slightly crooked canine.

"Not a deer, a *beast*," she replied.

The barking grew closer again. Quick as a flash, Eleri scaled the nearest tree and peered out into the distance from her perch. She scanned the horizon for only a moment before pointing to the east.

"I see it," she called down to Clara and Sioned. "The Questing Beast is just over the next ridge, headed this way."

Suddenly, Eleri's facial expression changed into one of concern.

"It's headed this way *very quickly!*"

As Eleri said this, she dropped from the branch she was on back to the ground. Just as she landed, Clara and Sioned heard the sounds of something crashing through the brush towards them, in addition to the sounds of barking dogs.

The three women scrambled back towards the road. Just as they made it back to the cobbled street, the Questing Beast burst forth from the treeline behind them. Its legs were strong and shaped like a deer's, propelled forward by the haunches of a lion. The Questing Beast had the body of a leopard but with a serpent's form starting at the neck. The snake head undulated, swinging side to side sinuously as if considering each of the women in turn. Hungry, territorial, or aggressive for some other unknown reason, its body language made it clear the beast was on the hunt.

"Have no fear, I'll keep you safe," Eleri said calmly, which made Clara snort in disbelieve and fear. The size difference between the Questing Beast and Eleri alone made the statement seem ridiculous to her.

Eleri placed herself between the Questing Beast and her companions, one hand on the hilt of her sword but not drawing it yet. This movement drew its full attention, and it focused in on Eleri alone. The Questing Beast's forked tongue flicked through the air experimentally. Its snake head was still as it stared but the serpentine neck undulated constantly. The Questing Beast took a tentative step forward. Eleri's face showed no sign of fear, but her hand shifted from resting on the hilt of her sword to holding the grip in readiness.

The sound of barking had subsided somewhat, and now the women could hear the faint hissing sound that came from the snake head. Eleri used her left hand to signal to the Clara and Sioned behind her back, silently urging them to remain calm and still. Even this small movement further agitated the defensive beast. It opened its maw, showing off long, thick fangs, and let out a sharp, loud hiss.

Sioned, spooked by this sudden threat display, bolted. Clara gave a startled shout and took off after her. They barely made it a few steps before the Questing Beast lunged after them, the sound of braying dogs as loud as if a hunting pack was truly on their heels. Its jaws snapped around empty air just behind Sioned's fleeing back—and probably would have caught her if the beast hadn't had to angle its body around Eleri.

The force with which the Questing Beast lunged forward knocked Eleri to the ground, caught up as she was by the joint between the beast's neck and shoulder. Eleri swiftly found herself underneath the trampling feet of the beast. She brought her hands to her face to protect it, but the Questing Beast was more concerned with the fleeing prey than the small one underfoot. It was only a pace or two behind the fleeing women, leaving Eleri on the road.

Bruised but undeterred, Eleri stood. She did not hesitate a second, instead immediately took off in pursuit of the others. Her booted feet kicked up dust from the dry road, and soon she was closing in on the Questing Beast. Sioned and Clara led them through the woods and off the trails Eleri knew well.

It was a flight of fear, obviously, as there was no reason for the women to flee into the darker, older sections of these woods. This was the forest of legends, where evil enchanters once roamed looking for knights to fool and monsters of all sorts lurked. Even as the memories of this time passed into myth, people still avoided this part of the woods. Although Eleri knew she had left behind a bright, sunny day, inside the forest felt cold, dark, and foreboding. Still, the strange party sped onwards.

Just as the Questing Beast lunged again to bite at Clara, Sioned tripped and, in falling, brought Clara down with her. Again, the Beast's mouth closed around air, and it hissed lowly in disappointment. There was little time for the women to examine what Sioned had tripped on, instead Clara focused on hauling herself and Sioned upright as the Questing Beast closed in on them.

From her position at the back of the group, Eleri had enough time to look ahead and see what had caused Sioned to fall. It was a large piece of stone rubble, laying half-buried in the overgrown grass. She altered her course slightly, coming at the stone block straight on rather than to the side as Sioned, Clara, and the Questing Beast had done. Eleri planted her front foot firmly on the block and used it as a springboard, jumping at the Questing Beast.

She managed to wrap her arms around its neck, and hung on tightly as the beast ran, then realised its new position and started trying to buck her off.

Now that the Questing Beast was no longer chasing them, Sioned and Clara slowed slightly and looked around. The bleak atmosphere of the woods around them was frightening, and Sioned clung to Clara's sleeve. Just as Clara was about to say something to try to comfort the other woman, Sioned's face lit up. "Look!" She cried. "A castle!"

Clara turned to see where Sioned was pointing and saw the ruins of an old castle half-hidden in the gloom. It was in disrepair, with one tower crumbled and large holes in the outer defenses, but the main structure of the castle seemed largely intact. The two made for the castle's door while the Questing Beast was still distracted.

As they peeked around the edge of the old wooden door, they saw Eleri clinging to the Questing Beast, unable to get the momentum needed to swing her leg over its back, or to get her feet to reach the ground to drag against the dirt and slow the beast down. Still, Eleri wrestled with it, until the Questing Beast gave up on its pursuit to focus on its unwanted passenger.

When the Questing Beast stopped running and put its back to the castle doors, Eleri finally slid from its neck. She stood facing the beast, panting heavily, and drew her sword. She held it firmly in her hand but kept the actual blade pointing down at the ground. The Questing Beast hissed again, and the sound of barking dogs nearly deafened Eleri.

With slow, cautious movements, Eleri tried to move around the beast's body, but it snapped at her whenever she drew too close. Suddenly, she feinted to the left and when the Questing Beast lunged after her, it lost its footing on another piece of castle debris. Eleri, already swerving to the right, used this to pass around the beast and run hard to the castle door. As she passed through it, Clara and Sioned shoved hard at the old wood and forced the rusty hinges to close the door.

Eleri coughed lightly as she took in their new surroundings. There was broken furniture everywhere, and a large hole in the roof of the entry hall, but other than that the castle would make a suitable shelter. It was only midday, but as Eleri could hear the Questing Beast prowling about outside, she suggested they make their camp for the night. The sounds of the beast, still intent on catching its prey—especially now that they were firmly within its natural hunting grounds—could be heard well into the night.

As they laid out their sleeping gear—Sioned picking her way through the ruined castle with a look of mild disgust on her face—Clara brought out some of their bread and cheese to make a simple meal. It was a quiet affair, as they each recovered from their recent scare.

Finally, as Eleri was looking over her maps to regain her bearings, she broke the silence.

"Strangely enough, I think ending up here may have been a bit of a shortcut. It's not the usual path I take, but it may save us a few days of travel."

Sioned smiled at this, but Clara looked pensive.

"You've said before that you take people to Gryphon's Keep sometimes," Clara began. "But you never explained why. What do you get out of this?"

Eleri laughed lightly. "Usually, it's just me making a pest of myself—the Elders and I have a contentious relationship at best. This time, though, I have... some questions I'd like to ask them. I consider myself a bit of a researcher, and they are the experts in the field of magic."

Eleri decided to leave out the magnitude of her questions. As anxious as she was about the decline of magic, she didn't want to worry Sioned and Clara if she didn't have to. Besides, Eleri was using this trip to the Keep as a distraction from her own concerns as well as an excuse to travel there.

"Don't you think making a nuisance of yourself will make the Elders not want to help you?" Sioned asked, a touch of apprehension in her voice.

"I already find them terribly unhelpful, honestly," Eleri said with a shrug. "It's part of why I dislike them so much. Those who claim to be an authority and refuse to help the people they oversee are unworthy of their positions, in my mind. They'll help me, or they won't, but at least I'll be able to go through their library when I'm there."

Clara's face fell. "Unhelpful...?" she asked, more to herself than anyone else.

"If you anger them, they're likely to prevent you from using their books." Sioned told Eleri primly.

Eleri grinned impishly. "They can sure try."

Chapter Eight

Eleri was curled up, resting her back against her pack, with her notebook in her hands. She wasn't really reading it, but it gave her the illusion of being busy. Originally, Eleri had pulled it out to refresh her memory on any important magical landmarks they'd pass on their way to Gryphon's Keep—their detour the day before had thrown them a little off course. However, Sioned had immediately used her 'distraction' to continue trying to get to know Clara better. She'd told Eleri that she'd seen Clara around Oldawynn so frequently that Sioned couldn't help but be intrigued by her, despite the lingering reservations the blonde woman seemed to hold.

It was likely Sioned would succeed, at least to some degree. There was little chance of privacy or seclusion on that night, as the three young women were camped out in the forest. It was their third night on the road, and the first that they were sleeping outside. This arrangement didn't bother Clara or Eleri, but Sioned seemed to be having some trouble adjusting to the harsher conditions.

Eleri didn't find it that terrible. The autumn weather was still warm enough to be comfortable, even at night. The drought meant that there was an unusual lack of rain for that time of year, plus tall, mature trees all around them that kept any wind from being too noticeable. It was actually very lovely, spending a few hours surrounded by tall conifer trees and their newly orange counterparts.

Eleri cast a glance towards the fire. Clara sat stirring a stew, giving quiet, quick answers to Sioned's flurry of questions. She was very reserved, true, but Clara didn't seem to actually mind Sioned hovering around her. Eleri would even say that, despite the strangely embarrassed expression and short replies, Clara seemed to follow Sioned's every move with both her eyes and body. Even now, Clara tracked their companion, either by watching her every move or by subtly turning her body towards Sioned.

It seemed a little strange to Eleri, who would have found all that attention overwhelming, but she let it pass without comment. Sioned and Clara were both older than her and capable of navigating relationships themselves. Besides, thought Eleri, there was no need for intervention when neither of them were overtly uncomfortable with their dynamic.

"So, Clara, the last thing I've been wondering about you is why you want to visit the Keep so much," Sioned declared, finally taking a seat next to the fire.

Clara stilled in response. She narrowed her eyes, but kept her sour expression directed at the pot of stew. It was an expression Clara had never used in conjunction with Sioned. She opened and closed her mouth a few times, looking for the words she wanted to say.

"They... they say that the Elders can take away your magic, if you don't want it."

Sioned startled almost comically, gaping at Clara with wide eyes. Clara blushed a brilliant red. Eleri peeked over the top of her book, now more interested in their conversation.

"Give it up? Are you crazy?" Sioned exclaimed. She ignored Clara's glare and continued:

"There are so many people *desperate* for magic, either to have or to use, and you'd want to give that gift up?"

Privately, Eleri agreed with Sioned, but the dark, angry look on Clara's face kept her mouth shut. The blonde slammed the spoon down, making it clang jarringly against the edge of the stew pot.

"Desperate for another reason to think I'm a freak, you mean!" Clara shouted. "Everyone always knew I was different, and then passing the Trials as an adult rather than a child cemented it!"

At some point, Clara had risen to her feet, and now stood over Sioned. It took a moment of heavy breathing after her outburst, but suddenly Clara realised her position, and the shocked look on

Sioned's face. Her posture slumped, despondent rather than angry.

"I... I'm sorry... I don't know what came over me..."

With that, Clara fled into the woods.

Eleri watched her go; it was still fairly light out and Clara was an adult who appeared to be able to handle herself. Besides, loud noises were not Eleri's favourite thing, and she needed a moment to centre herself.

So did Sioned, evidently. She, too, was breathing heavily, and had leaned back on her elbows when Clara had jumped up. For a moment there was a heavy silence in their little clearing.

"I suppose there's no point in pretending I didn't hear that," Eleri said.

She put her notebook to the side and tucked her legs neatly underneath her. Sioned, on the other hand, curled herself into a little ball, her eyes looking a little watery. When Sioned made no move to answer, Eleri shuffled forward, taking up the spoon and stirring the stew. It would do nothing for their humour if dinner was burnt, too. It looked good enough, so Eleri moved it away from the hottest part of the flame, and covered it with the pot's lid to keep the heat in.

"I didn't mean to upset her," Sioned whispered.

"I know."

"I just want to be friends."

"I know."

Sioned didn't say anything else, just buried her head in her arms. Eleri gripped her shoulder bracingly for a moment. With no other ideas of how to soothe the situation, Eleri set about making a pot of tea for them to share.

It took no time at all for the water to be heated, and soon they were drinking the tea. Or, at least, Eleri was. Sioned mostly stared into her cup, lost in thought.

The sun was truly beginning to set, and both women were starting to look over at the direction Clara had left in more frequently. Just as Sioned set her still-full cup down and opened her mouth, Clara came back into the clearing, looking tired.

Eleri could see the way that Sioned's legs twitched. Undoubtedly, she wanted to leap up and fawn over Clara, but she restrained herself. Clara saw it, too, and gave a half-hearted smile.

When she came close enough, Eleri poured Clara a cup of tea as well, and received a soft *thank you* in return. Clara hovered anxiously above them, taking small steps towards then away from Sioned. Eleri, seeing this, arranged herself so that she took up all the space on her side of the fire as best she could with her small frame. It earned her a frown from Clara, but the blonde stopped dithering and sat next to Sioned.

Clara opened her mouth, but was cut off by Sioned, who uncoiled from her ball like a spring.

"I'm sorry, Clara!" Sioned made a strange, aborted movement, but Clara correctly saw what it was meant to be and pulled Sioned into a hug. Sioned immediately tightened her grip on Clara in a way that looked vaguely painful to Eleri.

"I'm sorry, too, I shouldn't have blown up at you like that. I know it's a weird thing to want to do," Clara answered, speaking mostly into Sioned's dark hair.

"A little," Sioned giggled tearfully. "And it makes me really curious, but I can try not to pester you if you don't want to share."

Clara shrugged. Or she shrugged as much as she could while Sioned clung to her, and blushed when she realised how close they were. With one last squeeze, Sioned let go of Clara, and put some distance between them again.

"For what it's worth, I don't think you're a freak," Sioned said as she wiped her eyes.

"I'm a freak," Eleri added conversationally, still lounging on the other side of the fire. "It's not so bad, really."

"That's not helpful," Sioned's voice was reproachful, but she was obviously fighting a smile.

Clara let out a half-strangled laugh, and smiled for the first time since she'd returned, so Eleri felt it had been the right thing to say. The three of them sat quietly for a little while. The atmosphere of their little camp had changed, though luckily there was no remaining tension. It was obvious that Clara was embarrassed, either by her outburst or her unusual plan, and she could barely face Sioned. It seemed that they had regressed to how they had been in Oldawynn, with Clara always shying away from the other girl.

Sioned was also affected. She was much quieter and had returned to her curled-up position. Instead of loudly chatting with both Clara and Eleri she kept to herself, still staring into her full cup of tea, which was most assuredly cold by now.

Eventually, Clara noticed the stew pot and peeked inside. When she saw that it was untouched, she pulled out the bowls and spoons and dished up dinner. It was hard for Eleri to eat normally once she had the first bite, for she realised how hungry she was; the stew was also still piping hot, and Eleri spared a thought for how well-made Sioned's cookware was.

They ate in silence. It was now well and truly dark out, and Eleri was ready to put this strange evening to rest. When the other two had finished eating, she collected their bowls and took them to the nearby stream to wash them. Eleri came back to camp to find that Sioned and Clara had already laid out their bedrolls and were readying themselves for sleep. It was a little odd, considering that they usually stayed up later than Eleri, but then again, it was usually to chat with each other.

After finishing the last few tasks before they could all comfortably and safely sleep, Eleri also put out her bedroll and laid down. She was just beginning to drift off when she heard Clara speak.

"My family... didn't understand me. When I was young, they always tried to fit me into a box, make me be what they thought I should be."

Clara sighed. Even in the dark, it was clear that she was fussing with her blanket nervously. Eleri rolled onto her back and stared up at the stars, tracing the constellations in her mind. Neither she nor Sioned said anything.

"I was tested as a child for magic and failed," Clara continued, her voice soft but filled with hurt. "Another disappointment for my parents there. But when I became an adult, I decided to stop hiding who I was. I changed my hair, my clothes, even my name, and my parents were furious. And as soon as I did, I started showing signs of magic—that's why I was tested again and passed as an adult."

Sioned got up and dragged her bedroll closer to Clara. The three of them usually slept spaced out around the fire, but now Sioned positioned herself right beside Clara. As soon as Sioned was close enough to touch, Clara hid her face in her hands.

Sioned gently reached out and peeled Clara's hands from her face. She held them tenderly in her own.

"Your family doesn't deserve you," she told Clara firmly. Clara tried to take her hands back, but Sioned held fast. "Hey, no. There's no need to hide. I don't really know the details, but I can't believe anyone could find fault in you."

There was something so earnest on Sioned's face that Clara was helpless to do anything but nod. That seemed to pacify Sioned, who, with one final squeeze to Clara's hands, laid down beside the other woman. Once they were both tucked in, Sioned reached out, grasped Clara's shoulder, and rubbed it comfortingly.

"You'll find the right people for you one day. And hey, worse comes to worst, I'll just bring you home with me!" Sioned laughed. Clara gave out a strange squeak. She put her hands in her face again, but this time Sioned didn't notice or reach for them.

"Don't you think your family would be annoyed if you brought home a stranger instead of researching at Gryphon's Keep?" Clara's voice was somewhat muffled by her palms, but still intelligible.

"Not at all!" Sioned laughed. "They want me to be happy and all, but they don't really understand why I'd need to leave home to do that. I have a big family, and we all mostly stay close and work together. I'm sure they'd be thrilled if I came back earlier than expected."

Clara hummed and Sioned gave her one last gentle pat on the shoulder before retracting her hand. There was a beat of silence for a moment before they seemed to remember that it wasn't just the two of them alone in the clearing.

"What about you, Eleri? You still seem a little young to be travelling by yourself."

Sioned's question made Eleri crinkle her nose in distaste. She'd hoped the other two women would have been so wrapped up in their discussion that they wouldn't think to ask about her home life.

"My mother didn't want me. I haven't lived with her since I was six years old," Eleri said simply.

Clara sucked in a sharp breath, and Sioned jerked upright into a sitting position. Eleri felt her eyes boring a hole in the side of her head, but kept staring resolutely at the night sky.

"And... your father?" Clara asked tentatively.

"Dead. Before I was born."

"Oh, um," Sioned started awkwardly. It was clear she was struggling with what to say.

"Don't," Eleri told her. "Don't worry about it."

Over the cooling embers, Clara gave Eleri a sympathizing look. It was expected after Clara had shared what she had, and it was somewhat comforting. Sioned still looked like she wanted to say something. She was still sitting up, staring intently at Eleri. For her part, Eleri said nothing, content to wait Sioned out in silence.

Finally, after a few minutes, Clara reached out and guided Sioned into laying back down. It was a stiff movement, as Sioned was unsure if she really wanted to, but Clara began talking to her in low tones that Eleri couldn't hear. Whatever Clara said soothed

Sioned enough for her to acquiesce and go to bed, but Eleri knew that the conversation was far from over.

61

Sioned enough for her to acquiesce and go to bed, but Eleri knew that the conversation was far from over.

Chapter Nine

Eleri was the first one up. Eleri was always the first one up, but she had risen early even by her standards, unable to sleep after last night's conversation. By the time Sioned and Clara had disentangled themselves from their blankets, and each other, Eleri had tea and porridge ready.

While she waited for them to finish their morning toilet, she poked aimlessly at the fire with a long stick. Sioned made an effort to catch her eye as she served herself breakfast, but Eleri deliberately avoided the other girl's gaze. Clara had to gently steer Sioned away by the elbow to stop her from hovering over Eleri.

As the other two ate, Eleri brushed, plaited, and tied back her hair; it was a meditative act, one that both felt good and gave her something to focus on. It was another oddly silent meal for them, though Sioned kept looking at both Clara and Eleri with sad eyes. It was a little stifling, and Eleri was glad when Sioned left to do the dishes.

When Sioned had returned and they had packed up all their supplies, Eleri pulled a map from her belt and held it out for the other two.

"We're on track to make it to the Gryphon's Keep in roughly two days, if all goes well as we pass through the Forest of Yor," she said.

"What could go wrong in the Forest of Yor?" asked Clara.

"Oh, the Forest of Yor is just a high magic concentrate area. So you're more likely to encounter something supernatural there than in a regular forest."

"My dad says it's more dangerous, but the resources in there are more valuable, too," Sioned added. "Some of the merchants and vendors we deal with refuse to go in there, and the ones that do charge more because of all the hazards."

"'All of the hazards?' What do you mean by hazards?" Clara asked, sounding nervous.

That stopped Sioned short, and she also started to look nervous as she thought more about it. Eleri waved a hand dismissively.

"It's only dangerous if you stray from the path or pick a fight with something stronger than you." She was focused on rerolling the map, but when she looked up and saw Clara and Sioned's expressions, her face fell. "It's the only way to the Keep, otherwise we would have gone around. Stay alert, though, we're almost there."

"Are you sure? It looked like just a small area on the map. It would probably add a couple days, but we could go around," Sioned asked, pointing at the map that was back in Eleri's belt.

"I have to agree," Clara said. "If it's because of money, I can't imagine anyone wouldn't pay more to go around safely. Or that your clients would pay you at all if you get them injured."

"*Money* is the least of my concerns." Eleri corrected; her nose crinkled in annoyance. "And perhaps I wasn't clear enough; we can't go around the Forest of Yor to get to Gryphon's Keep, because Gryphon's Keep is *in* the Forest of Yor."

Sioned bit her lip, looking more and more nervous by the second. Clara, too, was obviously less than thrilled, though her upset now seemed to be directed at Eleri.

"Are you absolutely sure you know where the Keep is?" Clara demanded.

"Absolutely." Eleri was the shortest of the three girls by far, but she stood firm and straight against Clara, meeting the blonde's gaze head on.

"It's just, well, why would they build such an important place in such a dangerous area?" Sioned broke in timidly, looking between the other two.

"Why would they have the centre of magic research in such a magic-heavy area?" Eleri rolled her eyes. "Can't think!"

Clara gave Eleri a sharp shove. "Don't talk to her like that!"

Sioned gasped and came forward to put herself between Clara and Eleri. Eleri let her, and even took a step back to give more space. Clara and Sioned stood close together, watching Eleri for her next move. Sioned looked distressed at the turn the conversation had taken, while Clara just looked annoyed. Eleri kept her face as neutral as possible and gave a deliberately blasé shrug.

"The fact of the matter is, Gryphon's Keep is inside of the Forest of Yor. I will lead you there, but you are not obligated to follow. Go home if you want. It makes no difference to me."

With that, Eleri spun sharply on her heel, plait flying behind her, and marched determinedly out of the clearing. There was only a moment where she heard nothing, then a pair of hurried footsteps came up just behind her. Eleri did not look back, nor slow her fast pace. Rather, she pretended there was nothing unusual about her circumstances, and fell back on her default of humming to herself as she travelled.

The path they were taking was not that difficult. It was heavily trafficked, enough that even the grass and moss had been worn down to dirt. It was obvious that the trees were regularly maintained, and only a few branches—recently broken—hung down in their way. Without having to maneuver around overgrown foliage, Eleri was able to keep up a brisk pace for the whole morning. Sometimes she caught snatches of Sioned and Clara's conversation behind her, but it was mostly forced-sounding small talk about Sioned's father's trading in the region, or comments on the scenery.

It was another annoyingly warm day for autumn, and Eleri was glad her hair was contained. The back of her neck was beginning to sweat, even without a heavy layer of dark hair covering it. The sun was high above them in the sky, shining with some ferocity, and Eleri occasionally had to use her hand to shade her eyes to see better. It was one moment such as this, where Eleri paused to check she was on the correct path, when the other two women finally caught up to her.

"Eleri!" Sioned panted, her cheeks even darker than usual. "We've been walking for hours; can't we take a break and eat something?"

"Yeah, and I think you've made your point," agreed Clara, who was also flushed and had a ring of sweat around her collar.

Eleri tilted her head, regarding the blonde with some confusion.

"My point?" she asked.

Before anyone could say anything else, however, Eleri's stomach let out a loud growl. Surprised, she put a hand to it—Eleri hadn't even realised she was hungry at all, much less the intensity of it.

It was decided that they would walk back to a clearing they had passed not five minutes ago and make camp for lunch. Sioned and Clara led the way, and Eleri trailed after them, rummaging in her pack. The pair of them were already starting to build a fire when Eleri sat down, which she hadn't planned on, but figured she could use a cup of tea if there was heat available. Her arm was still stuck in her bag, now in her lap, so she simply added the tin cup and package of tea to her mental list of things to feel for. As she found them, she drew out the tea, a block of cheese, her water-skin, and some bread.

When she looked up, Eleri caught Sioned staring at her again. Eleri tilted her head back at her, which Sioned took as an invitation to begin a conversation.

"How do you fit all that in that little bag?" Sioned asked, gesturing at the items resting on Eleri's crossed legs.

It was a fair question, Eleri thought, looking at her pack. It wasn't as big as Sioned or Clara's, about the width of her own torso. It fit comfortably on her belt, didn't impede her movements, and held all she needed.

"I suppose I've always been good at packing." Eleri said, holding her pack so that Sioned could see into the opening.

Clara snorted. "You fit all that in there, and the bread doesn't come out squished? It's got to be magic."

"It's not. I didn't buy an enchanted pack; I bought a star-patterned one. Trust me, I paid enough to know exactly what I ordered, not a penny more." Eleri put her hand back in the pack, rooting around for her teacup.

"Eleri," Clara said impatiently. "Your arm is in that bag up to your elbow. You regularly put a bedroll bigger than the pack into the pack. It's magic, and I don't know why you're denying it."

Eleri looked down at her arm with a blank expression. It was true that she had most of her limb in the bag, much deeper than possible, based on the outside dimensions of her travel pack. But she also knew that she had never taken the bag to a mage to be enchanted like that.

"I don't know what to tell you." She shrugged, finally removing the teacup.

She set about the motions of making tea, and then went to prepare her lunch.

"I get that you're ashamed of not having magic or whatever, but I don't get why you'd lie about getting someone else to use it for you," Clara pressed on.

Perhaps it was some lingering tension from the morning, or being doubted for a second time that day, but Eleri did something quite uncharacteristic then. She fastened the cover of her pack, then tossed it at Clara and Sioned. It was Clara who caught it, and she glared at Eleri, even though it had been a very soft and slow throw.

"Check it, if it bothers you so much," Eleri told them with a deliberately casual and pleasant voice.

Sioned and Clara sat for a moment, dumbfounded. This was not the turn they had expected the conversation to take. Sioned recovered first, and gently pulled Eleri's bag into her lap. After getting a nod of approval from Eleri, Sioned pulled a thin leather cord from the inside of her shirt, which had a thumbnail sized golden crystal dangling at the end.

Eleri tried not to stare too much, but mentally catalogued that the conduit Sioned needed to access her magic was a crystal. While some people believed that conduits were tied to a mage's personality, Eleri didn't hold to that theory. Still, it was an interesting tidbit of information. Eleri briefly wondered if Sioned would be able to produce a grym to replace the one she'd used up.

Sioned held the crystal in one hand and placed the other on the cover of Eleri's bag. She closed her eyes, said something too quiet for Eleri to hear, and there was a brief, soft glow of gold from inside her fist. Then Sioned did it a second time.

"She's right. I can't feel any specific spell that would enlarge the inside," Sioned said with a shrug, though she still looked confused.

Eleri opened her mouth, but was swiftly cut off by Clara, who sounded a little too victorious.

"No *specific* spell? Does that mean you sense other magic on the bag?"

Again, Sioned shrugged, but she seemed more sure of her conclusions now. She held out Eleri's bag for Clara to take, which she did.

"I guess, yeah. But it doesn't feel like a spell or enchantment that I know. More... shapeless, I think."

Clara, as it turned out, used a wand as a conduit. She removed it from her sleeve and performed a similar check on Eleri's bag. Once it was confirmed that there was no enlargement charm on Eleri's bag, she and Sioned devolved into a conversation about the 'shapeless' magic they had felt.

Eleri tired of the conversation quickly. She leaned forward and reclaimed her bag. When it was back in her possession, she pulled two of the gryms from it. She rattled them around in her hand, making them clink against each other, then held them out for inspection when Sioned and Clara turned to look at her.

"I carry a handful of these with me at all times, for emergencies. They may be what you're sensing from within the bag."

That was enough to satisfy Clara, as she nodded seriously. She then returned her attention to the fire and whatever food she was preparing. Sioned frowned at Eleri for a moment longer, then she made a move, as if to ask for the magic baubles.

Clara called for Sioned's help, and the moment was broken. Once Sioned looked away, Eleri replaced the gryms in their pouch on her pack, then set about fixing her own simple lunch. She finished eating before Sioned and Clara, as she required no cooking. When she was done, and had cleaned up after herself, she took a drink of water, swished it around in her mouth, and spat it out on the ground, a respectable distance from the other two.

"What was that?" Sioned shouted, more than a little surprised.

Clara said nothing, but her face made it clear that what Eleri had done was also a somewhat distasteful mystery. Eleri couldn't help the laugh that bubbled out of her. She waved a hand dismissively, and returned to where her pack was.

"Strange, I know," she told them.

Then she once again reached into her bag and withdrew a long, flat case. Eleri got herself situated on the ground, looking for the most comfortable position. As she did this, she heard Clara mutter to Sioned that the case was longer than the bag Eleri had pulled it out of. Eleri ignored this, seeing no point in continuing that discussion, and opened the case.

Inside was a finely-crafted flute. Not only was it well-formed, but it had been lightly engraved with depictions of constellations all over its body. After she had prepared it, Eleri lifted it in mock salute towards her companions and lifted it to her mouth.

The first note out of the flute was clean and clear, but Eleri pulled the flute away and readjusted it anyway. When she was sure of her position, she immediately dove into a jaunty little tune. Eleri played the whole time Sioned and Clara ate and packed up her flute with care when it was time for them to get back to their travels.

Chapter Ten

"Have you played the flute long, Eleri?"

Sioned and Clara had been chatting quietly, but now the dark-haired girl raised her voice and directed her question to Eleri. Some of the tension of the morning had bled out during lunch, even considering the brief argument about Eleri's pack. The twin soothing effects of food and cheerful music were likely responsible for the amelioration of the general mood. Eleri hummed in consideration, partly in response to Sioned's question and partly due to being lost in her own thoughts.

"No, not long. Only a few years, really," Eleri said, looking back at the pair over her shoulder. "I started learning the piano, then moved to the guitar—my favourite—and picked up the flute for something a little more...portable."

She wasn't walking as quickly as she had been that morning, as she had let go the majority of her irritation at her travelling companions. This made it easy for Sioned to come up beside Eleri and bring Clara along with her by her hand. Sioned wore an expression of curiosity.

"Three instruments? How ever did you find the time?"

"And singing!" Clara added. "She sings well, too. Don't forget."

Eleri laughed, delighted. She spun so she was walking backwards, facing Sioned and Clara with the biggest smile they had ever seen on her face.

"Goddesses above! You are going to make me blush with all these compliments!" Then she shrugged, still beaming. "I suppose I just have a talent for music, I always know what note I'm hearing, and I can sing, or play, any one at a moment's notice."

It was slightly cooler that afternoon, as the wind had picked up a little and brought some cloud cover with it. The more bearable temperatures certainly helped the women's tempers, and they spent the better part of their time laughing and chatting as Sioned and Clara tried to stump Eleri with surprise musical note requests. Not only did Eleri never falter—though she did sometimes scold them good-naturedly about picking a note outside of her range— but Clara was also delighted to learn that Eleri had a head for remembering songs in their entirety. It didn't seem to matter if Eleri had heard it once or three dozen times, she was able to recall both the tune and any associated lyrics with no issues.

They spent some time singing merrily, with Eleri leading and Clara and Sioned joining when they could. It was a good way to keep their morale up, too, as the forest around them had grown denser and more difficult to navigate. There was something of a path to follow, but it was hard to see and often intersected by dead fall the women had to climb over.

The clouds above them continued to grow and darken, so Clara suggested that they make camp earlier than usual to better prepare for what was surely to be a rainy night. In Sioned's supplies, she had a large piece of canvas, which the three of them used to build a sort of shelter. Suspended between the trees, with one side of the canvas hanging down as a windbreak, there was just enough space for the girls to cram their bedrolls in, all tucked up beside each other. It would be much closer quarters than they usually had, but the proximity would help keep them warm during the night.

It was too soon for supper, especially considering their relatively late lunch. Sioned and Clara sat on the bedrolls, playing some sort of card game, while Eleri flitted about between the trees. She was jotting down notes and occasionally pressed a leaf or flower between the pages.

"What are you doing, Eleri?" Clara called to her when Eleri was almost out of sight of their little shelter.

Eleri stood from where she was crouched over a bit of moss and regarded Clara with a tilted head. Then she came a little closer so that they need not have their conversation shouted through the trees. She held her little notebook in front of her chest so Clara, and now Sioned as well, could see it.

"This little book is my most steadfast companion," she told them, as she ran a fond hand along the spine. "I have had it since I was little, and I fill it not just with my research, but also with anything that catches my fancy. Flowers, recipes, the best place to buy a tart in any town I visit. A thought I want to remember, or a score of music I'm working on."

Sioned clambered out of the shelter. When she approached Eleri, hands out to take the notebook, the younger woman balked a little. After examining Sioned's face, Eleri gently placed the careworn book in Sioned's hands, who held it just as reverently as Eleri had. Sioned gave the book a brief flip-through, but not slow enough to see more than an inkling of what was on the pages.

"Since you were little, huh? It must be full to the brim by now."

"Almost," Eleri said with a smile. "Yet I still always manage to find a fresh page when I need it. I suppose I'll need a new one soon, but I don't know what I'll do when this little notebook is gone..." Her voice turned slightly wistful at the end.

"It does seem very full," Sioned agreed, handing it back. "Come sit with us a while, tell us about it."

Sioned grabbed Eleri by the wrist and dragged her back to the shelter. Clara shuffled over, making enough space for the two to join her. It wasn't Eleri's ideal arrangement, but she gamely tucked herself under the shelter, and close to Sioned's side. The older two were all but cuddled against each other and seemed more comfortable than Eleri felt.

Eleri felt a sudden burst of self-consciousness but flipped through her notebook to find a page with song lyrics and music notes on it. She thought it was a safe place to start, based on Sioned and Clara's reactions to her musical ability earlier in the day. The first one she drew their attention to was a snatch of a song about voyagers in space who came home to find that the world they returned to was older than they were. It always made her cry, thinking of those people coming home to their grown grandchildren.

The young women then flipped through the pages, pointing and exclaiming in delight at the pressed flowers or pretty little pamphlets pressed in the book. After enjoying Eleri's keepsakes, Clara reached out to touch the younger girl's wrist.

"You said you have research in here as well? What kind of things do you study?"

Eleri twisted her ring. It had obviously come up that she had no magic of her own, and while Sioned and Clara were nice enough, some mages were oddly offended when a non-magic user studied magic.

"Well..." Eleri said slowly, searching through the pages of her book. "I do have an interest in magic..."

Clara said nothing, and Sioned gave an encouraging hum, so Eleri decided to delve in a little deeper. Finding the page she was looking for, Eleri pointed at a hand drawn diagram which showed a selection of different orbs, each with different auras, and their individual characteristics neatly labelled.

"Look, these are all the result of the same light spell, but they manifest differently. Some scholars have argued that that is the result of the way the spell is cast, while others think that it is a reflection of the mage who performed the spell."

Eleri got increasingly excited the longer she spoke. Halfway through her explanation, she shifted onto her knees to be able to gesture better at her notes. Clara also leaned in to be able to see better. With her space being invaded, Sioned laid her head on Clara's shoulder.

"Eleri..." Clara started, very gently. "Isn't this outdated? I mean, no one ever even mentioned anything like this when I was getting my training."

Eleri visibly deflated at her words and sat back on her heels.

"Well, I suppose so. Magic is so limited these days, the way it's done is less important than the fact that it's done at all. Still," Eleri said, and gave a little self-deprecating shrug and a wry grin. "It's all theoretical for me, so I can focus on what I want to."

Clara grinned back, and Sioned pulled them both closer into a sort of half-hug.

"Theoretical or not, it is kinda interesting. I'd be okay with hearing more if you'd share," Sioned said, flipping to the next page. Rather than diagrams, it contained a list of spells with little annotations underneath each one.

"Ah! These are interesting little enchantments." Eleri's voice was filled with excitement again. "This builds off what we just talked about; they're different ways of finding out who cast a spell! If the individual mage affects the shape of the spell, you should be able to trace their magic back to them."

"Wow," Sioned whispered, more to herself than anything. "I never looked at magic this way; it's more intricate than I ever thought if you can pull it apart like this. D'you think that I could borrow some of your notes when we get to the Keep? I think I found what I want to research."

Eleri looked very pleased with Sioned's question.

"Of course! Although, you may get some weird looks about choosing such an 'antiquated' topic. Not much use delving deeper into magic if you can barely cast the spell." Eleri shrugged again. "Or so they tell me."

Sioned and Eleri discussed more, each growing more excited as they delved deeper into the unseen mysteries of magic. Sioned had lifted her head from Clara's shoulder, and Clara had taken up the same position but in reverse. She gamely endured the odd bumps and jolts as Sioned all but jumped around with happiness. The only time Clara flinched, despite the somewhat rough treatment, was when her long blonde hair got caught in Sioned's earring. This caused a brief pause in the discussion, as the two older women had to work together to untangle themselves.

The sun had started to set before Sioned and Eleri began to run out of steam. As their conversation was naturally winding down,

Clara extracted herself from the shelter, calling back to ask what Sioned needed to make dinner that night. As the blonde was sorting through their bags, there was a rustling sound from the bushes nearby. It sounded like a large disturbance; there were leaves shaking, branches breaking, and heavy footsteps. Clara and Eleri were immediately on high alert. With her wand drawn, Clara faced the direction of the noise, though her face was pale. Sioned tucked herself further under the shelter, eyes wide in fear, but raised her hand towards her necklace anyway.

Eleri wasted no time. She dove for her sword and strode determinedly towards the source of the sound. With a practice flick of her wrist, she twirled the blade into a low guard position and advanced on sure and soundless feet. She used her free arm to delicately part the branches in front of her and peered into the dim forest.

With a sharp gasp, Eleri drove her sword into the ground at her feet and all but leapt into the foliage.

"It's a person!" she shouted over her shoulder. "And they're injured too!"

Clara quickly re-sheathed her wand and hurried over. Between the two of them, they were able to support the badly hurt man and help him into their campsite. Sioned had crawled forward and used a spell to create a fire with a good bed of embers already glowing. She set some water to boil, then helped Eleri sort through their supplies for bandages as Clara settled the man into a seated position.

Eleri went to retrieve her sword and stood for a moment, staring out into the night. She heard no sign of pursuit, and the birds and insects chirped and buzzed merrily. It seemed whatever had attacked the man was no longer in the vicinity.

They had the man laid out next to the fire on his back, Sioned's jacket pillowed under his head. Clara was helping him drink slowly from another water-skin. Eleri dropped to her knees beside him and helped Sioned start cleaning his wounds with a cloth and the now-boiled water. As they wiped the blood from his face, he began to groan quietly. Clara had to quickly pull the water-skin away, afraid that he would start to choke.

The man blinked his eyes open and peered blearily at his surroundings. With an exceeding amount of effort, he managed to raise his head slightly, and grinned painfully when he saw the three women.

"Angels..." he said to himself, then closed his eyes and put his head back on his makeshift pillow.

Eleri couldn't help the sharp exhale of laughter she let out, and Sioned reached over the man to give her light shove to the shoulder. She ignored Sioned's remonstrating gaze, and instead gave the man two firm, but not unkind, slaps to the cheek. He forced his eyes open again at the contact.

"Hey," she started gently. "Stay awake, and tell us where you're injured."

"Chest... Shoulder..." he managed to whisper, gesturing vaguely at his left shoulder and pectoral with his free hand.

"Right. This may hurt." Eleri shifted to kneel over him, and carefully started to peel the layers of his clothes away from the area indicated.

As she pulled away the fabric of his coat and shirt, it became apparent that there were large, ragged tears in the material. Once Eleri and Sioned had the man's torso undressed, it was discovered that the rips in the fabric corresponded with three large gashes: a single deep, wide one that crossed the breastbone horizontally, and two thinner ones from the shoulder down over the man's collarbone.

Sioned moved Eleri's hands out of the way once most of the blood was cleaned from the man's chest. She removed her necklace and held it over the epicentre of the wounds with both hands. She held them there for a moment, then pulled back with a frown. She did that two more times, looking more and more distraught after each attempt. Finally, the man roused himself one more time to look at Sioned.

"Sorry, love, already tried magic. Didn't work for me, either."

Chapter Eleven

Clara and Sioned sat in stunned silence at the man's words. He gave a feeble cough, obviously in too much pain to continue speaking, and dropped his head back to the ground. Nothing more came from him but the occasional groan and laboured breathing.

Eleri's mouth twisted into dismayed moue, but she continued tending to the man without pause. After determining that there was little point in continuing to bathe his wounds, Eleri started to sort through the supplies the women had gathered, grabbing every bit of long, acceptably clean fabric available. One of them, her own dark cloak, she folded carefully and laid over the man's shoulder. Eleri held it in place with both hands, hoping to staunch some of the bleeding.

At the same time, Sioned and Clara had come together to discuss this new development. Clara knelt down, Sioned had twisted away from the patient, and they whispered rapidly between them. Eleri caught a brief mention of her name but tuned them out to focus on the man. His face had paled significantly since she and Clara had laid him by the fire. Eleri didn't notice that the conversation had shifted to include her until Clara reached over and poked her harshly in the arm. Eleri looked up with a glare.

"Eleri, Sioned and I want to use one of those gryms you showed us to help heal this man," Clara told her, still whispering to avoid disturbing the man.

Eleri gave a non-committal hum. If the magic here was as faded as in the villages she'd visited recently, an extra boost of magic would be wasted. Still, the life of this man may have depended on it, so she used one hand to gesture at her pack and quickly replaced it on the makeshift bandage.

"Bring my whole bag with you, please."

Clara nodded and rose from her kneeling position to do just that. Hands still applying pressure, Eleri gave the women directions on which pocket held the crystals. Sioned withdrew one, and she and Clara held hands, each holding their respective conduit, and attempted another healing spell as one.

As Eleri suspected, nothing happened beyond the strange liquidation of the grym. Sioned, who had been the one holding it, gave a shout of disgust and waved her hand around, flinging the multihued liquid around wildly.

"What happened?" Clara demanded, equally disgusted.

Sioned found a piece of cloth Eleri had rejected for being too small and used it to wipe her hand clean. Clara also cleaned her hand and offered it to Eleri, whose face had been caught in the spray. Eleri nodded her head towards the man's chest, where her hands were still occupied, so Clara put the cloth aside and the liquid stayed on Eleri's face, half-covering her smattering of freckles.

A strange burbling sound rose up from the man; it took Eleri a second to realise it was the man trying not to laugh at their antics. It made his shoulders shake, and even the minute movements seemed to bring pain. There was a glob of the bauble's fluid on his face as well, which had landed on his eye, so he only cracked the clean one open.

"Told you," he said breathlessly. "No magic."

Sioned looked devastated. Clara's expression cycled through a number of emotions but settled on anger. She looked between the puddle left on the grassy ground, and the man's face.

"How can there be no magic? I have magic, Sioned has magic, the *world* has magic, but this man is suddenly magic-proof or whatever? I honestly do not know what you are talking about, if—"

Clara's voice had been steadily rising in pitch throughout her little speech, and her words came out faster and faster. Sioned, uncharacteristically silent, had sat at Clara's feet, gripping her trouser leg with a white-knuckle grip. When Clara broke off, apparently unable to find the words she was looking for, she just stared at the man's still present wounds and soundlessly moved her mouth.

"It's not surprising, since magic is dying out and all. This isn't even the first time I've seen a grym fail," Eleri told them.

When she looked up to see the twin horrified faces of Sioned and Clara staring back at her, Eleri winced internally. Perhaps that was a too matter-of-fact way to break the news to them. Eleri tried again, consciously gentling her tone of voice.

"No need to worry, though, I'm sure the Elders are researching the phenomenon as we speak."

"No need to worry?!" shrieked Sioned, clutching somehow even tighter to Clara's clothes.

"Ah. Well." Eleri crinkled her nose, unsure of how she was going to salvage this one, especially since she herself was very worried about this. "At least worry about it after we help this man."

That was apparently an acceptable answer, as both Sioned and Clara calmed down enough to focus on the matter at hand.

"I have a sewing kit in my bag," Eleri mused. She looked to the man, who was still watching the proceedings with one eye. "I could stitch you up?"

Sioned sucked in a breath, but the man gave a minute nod.

"Are you sure about this?" asked Clara, looking both revolted and doubtful.

"I'm not sure we have any other choice," Eleri responded. "The kit is in my pack, it's a little silver tin with a bird on it. If you could pass it over, and, ah, yes, that's the one."

Eleri shifted to use her left forearm to hold the fabric down on the wound. She balanced her little tin on the man's chest and used her free hand to retrieve a needle and the thread with the best balance of thinness and tensile strength. She had to lean over the man awkwardly, but she managed to hold the needle in the flame of the campfire until it grew red-hot. Eleri shook it wildly, trying to cool it back down—and in hopes that the air would soothe her now burnt fingertips. When she deemed the metal to be ready, she threaded the needle and apologised quietly when her strange position ended up putting too much pressure on the man's chest.

Eleri sat back, removed her arm, and peeled the makeshift bandage away from the scratches as gently as she possibly could. She started with the deepest cut, and with steady hands made her first stitch. The man immediately jumped and gave out a strangled shout of pain.

"Clara, could you please hold his shoulders steady? And Sioned, see if you can't find something for him to bite down on."

There was a brief flurry of activity. Sioned rummaged through all their supplies and found a leather cuff of Clara's. They shared a kind of non-verbal communication, and Sioned brought the cuff forward. At the same time, Clara came to kneel near the head of the man and put her hands on both of his shoulders. She wasn't pressing down yet but was ready to. Sioned came and fit the leather cuff between the man's teeth, and then sat across from Eleri, nearer the man's knees.

The man had closed his eyes when the needle first punctured his skin, but he opened it again to look at Eleri and nod, allowing her to continue. Clara took the opportunity to clear the grym fluid from his other eye with her sleeve.

Eleri worked meticulously. There was a sort of practised speed to her actions, but she never rushed. Each stitch was placed with the utmost care, and Eleri remained fully focused on her task until all three wounds were sewn up. Clara, and eventually Sioned when the man's legs started to jerk, held him down, but Eleri still had to work with his flinches. Sioned kept up a steady stream of soothing words the entire time, but Eleri barely heard her.

When she finished, Eleri straightened her back with a loud pop. She stood, made her way over to their supplies, and washed her hands. Clara used the cloth and boiled water to give the man's wounds a final cleaning, then gently patted them dry. Meanwhile, Eleri searched her bag to find a clean, long skirt. It was one that she hadn't worn since washing, and that, plus the length of it, made it the perfect candidate for the final bandaging, even if Eleri was sad to see it go.

She sat back next to the man, who by now had spit out the leather cuff and was once again being gently fed water. Eleri set to tearing her skirt lengthwise, though she avoided making any of the buttons or other notions part of the bandages. In the end, the waistband of the skirt was left, and the rest had been made into long linen strips.

"Could you prop him up a little? I need to be able to wrap this around his chest," asked Eleri.

Clara, still kneeling at the man's head, pulled his shoulders onto her lap. It gave just enough clearance under his torso for a hand to pass underneath. In order to keep the bandages from picking up dirt, Sioned came forward to help Eleri. They took turns passing the fabric around the man, using their hands to shield it from the ground, until the wounds were adequately wrapped.

"Thank you..." the man whispered.

The women got him situated as comfortably as possible by the fire. Then, while Sioned started to make dinner, Clara and Eleri worked to shift their little shelter to cover the man as well. After a quick discussion, they decided it was best to cover the man in his entirety, so Eleri volunteered to be the one whose bedroll didn't fully fit under the canvas. She figured it made the most sense for the bottom of her bedroll to stick out, seeing as she usually slept curled up in a ball.

Dinner was a simple affair on account of their guest. Sioned had made a simple broth for him, and the rest of them had the same, with some potatoes and vegetables added in. Eleri provided some hard tack, which helped make the meal a little more filling for the women.

The rain they had been expecting finally started as they ate. The air was somber, and they took turns helping the man drink his broth. When they had all had their fill, Clara suggested leaving their dishes in the rain to be done in the morning. The women found themselves tucking into their bedrolls, partly to keep warm in the now dismal weather, and partly out of a lack of other options. They made sure to tuck any spare blankets they still had around the man, although he had already fallen asleep after he finished eating.

Close as they were, it was impossible for Eleri to ignore the pointed looks both Sioned and Clara were sending her way. They huddled together even closer, if that was even possible, and whispered between themselves, occasionally shooting Eleri strange looks. This was not an unusual experience in Eleri's life, despite being mildly irritating, so she left them to it. If they really had something to say, they would say it to her, or so she figured.

"Eleri. What did you mean earlier that magic is dying out?" Sioned asked, her voice firm and direct.

Sioned had previously mentioned that she had multiple younger siblings, and Eleri idly wondered if this was her 'big sister' voice. Eleri shrugged but didn't look at Sioned or Clara. Instead, she kept her eyes focused on her rings, which she twisted all one way, from first to pinkie finger, then back the opposite direction in reverse order.

Clara nudged Eleri's knee with her foot. That made her look up, and Eleri saw that Sioned and Clara sat side by side, staring her down with twin looks of admonition.

"You can't just say that and then not elaborate," Clara said.

A part of Eleri bristled at that. There was a strong streak of defiance in her that reared its head whenever she was told she 'had' to do something. In this instance, however, she swallowed it down. As mages, the decline of magic would affect Sioned and Clara's entire way of life, and Eleri could understand the frustration of being left out of the loop—and she wouldn't wish that on anyone.

"This is not the first time I've seen gryms fail, and they haven't all been mine," Eleri told them, back to looking at and playing with her rings. "I went to a magic pilgrimage site recently... and felt the magic leave the air."

Sioned sucked in a breath, her face ashen. Clara, on the other hand, looked less impressed. The blonde woman leaned back and crossed her arms.

"You 'felt' the magic leave the air? Really? Eleri, may I remind you that you don't have any magic of your own." Clara then raised a skeptical brow. "How would you feel anything to do with magic?"

Eleri kept her face carefully neutral; only the set of her jaw belayed her irritation.

"Well, you're no astronomer, but I think you'd notice if the sun went out. Even if you're not using it for calculations in your daily life," Eleri snarked.

Clara snorted derisively, clearly unimpressed with Eleri's metaphor. She told the younger girl so, and Eleri rolled her eyes.

"You might never think about the sun, but our society is based just as much on it as magic. The days, the years—regulated by the sun. The crops we eat, the material we use for clothes and shelter— grown by the sun. It's so entwined with our lives, just like magic is. It is the rhythms of the natural world made tangible, usable, for those with the gift. It is unthinkable to me that anyone with even an ounce of knowledge of magic wouldn't be able to feel it."

A flash of lightning tore through the sky, illuminating Eleri's face. In that brief moment, it seemed her eyes glowed a brilliant blue. Her gaze was already intense during her speech, but the strange lighting made her seem more so, in an almost otherworldly way. Then the light faded, and it was just Eleri again.

The moment had left Clara speechless, and Sioned, too. They simply sat there quietly. Eleri, more than worn out after her improvised doctoring and the conversation, tucked herself into her bedroll and curled up to sleep. Sioned did, too, but Clara sat up for a while, listening to the sounds of three sleeping people breathe, and thinking.

Chapter Twelve

When Clara opened her eyes, the day had already dawned. It was still a grey and drizzly morning, but weak sunlight drifted through the clouds to illuminate their campsite. Somewhere to her left, she could hear the sweet sounds of Eleri singing to herself softly. Cozy as she was, despite a burgeoning headache, Clara was tempted to burrow back into her wonderful pillow and go back to sleep. That is, until her pillow giggled lightly.

Clara shot upright and found that in the night she had ended up clinging to Sioned, with her head on the other woman's chest. When she saw Clara's shocked expression, Sioned laughed louder. Now free of Clara's weight, she also sat up,

"Your hair is so different from mine, all thin and fine. It tickled my nose," Sioned told Clara, still laughing.

By this time Eleri had stopped singing. To avoid showing Sioned how red her face was, Clara turned to see what her youngest companion was doing. Her bedroll had been folded and brought closer to the fire and was now being used to prop up the injured man, who was now awake. This added height gave him enough mobility to feed himself some porridge, which he did while wincing occasionally.

He looked well enough, though still pale and wane. His bandages looked slightly disturbed, but Clara assumed that was the result of Eleri checking for infection. When he caught Clara looking at her, he smiled and gave an odd little wave with his spoon.

"This is Charles," Sioned told Clara helpfully.

She had also packed up her bedroll since Clara had released her, and must have found a bit of privacy, as she had changed her clothes. Sioned unwrapped the bit of silk she wore at night to protect her hair and crawled over to where Eleri and Charles were. Not wanting to be the only one left in bed, Clara made quick work of her morning routine, somewhat awkwardly due to the small space under the shelter and her unwillingness to be rained on just yet.

"G'morning, Clara," Charles said as she helped herself to breakfast. "I want to thank you for your help last night. Without you ladies, I would have been a goner."

"I'm not sure I did much for you in the long run, but you're welcome."

"All so modest! The three of you each downplayed your part in my rescue, but obviously it was good enough to keep me on this Earth." Charles seemed delighted by their modesty. "Now, what's a group of pretty little things doing out here alone? This is the Forest of Yor, you know."

Based on what she had seen and felt when Charles first arrived, Clara was reasonably certain she was taller than him and was not so fond of being addressed as 'little.' Eleri, too, seemed less than impressed with Charles, since she crinkled her nose and decided that washing dishes in the rain was obviously more appealing than staying close.

"We're going to Gryphon's Keep!" Sioned told him, taking his now-empty bowl and passing it to Eleri.

The air chilled considerably at that, and it was not just because of the bought of wind that rattled through the tree branches above their heads. Charles adopted a bemused expression, looking between Sioned and Clara, and even trying to look over his shoulder at Eleri—but abandoned that movement when it pulled on his stitches.

"The Keep? I can't imagine you girls would have any business there. Besides, it's too dangerous! You must have heard of the dangers that lurk in Yor, and you can see what it did to me!" Charles gestured at his bandaged wounds.

"Eleri has a sword," Sioned defended, but she looked a little uncomfortable.

"And she knows how to use it," Clara broke in. "She knows the way to the Keep, too."

The defence of Eleri was only in part to convince Charles they knew what they were doing. Clara mostly wanted to remind Sioned that there was nothing to fear; she'd grown up surrounded by a big family on a rich merchant's estate and was sometimes nervous about the realities of travelling alone.

Charles smiled at the two of them, but it was brittle and cold. Clara had finished her porridge, but Eleri was clearly staying away from this discussion, so Clara held her bowl awkwardly in her lap. Eleri fluttered about in the rain, which, though light, was starting to truly dampen her clothes and hair.

"Miss Eleri has a sword and knows the way to the Keep... but she doesn't look like she's lived two decades. Are you sure you can trust her?"

Charles had identified Sioned as the weakest link. He placed a gentle hand on her knee, and leaned as close as his bandages would allow. It was obvious that Sioned's resolve was wavering, but just before she could speak, Eleri appeared holding her tin cup in one hand and a little knife in the other. She filled the cup with water that had been warming on the fire and all but shoved it unto Charles' hands.

"Here. It's willow bark and mint. Drink it for the pain." Eleri's words were clipped, as she stood there, looking damp and moody. It was a little much, Clara thought. As insulting as Charles sounded, he wasn't actually incorrect in his assessment; the path they were travelling on was dangerous and Eleri was very young. She would be lying if she said seeing Charles' wound didn't make her rethink their plans, but Clara was dedicated to reaching the Keep and returning to her normal life. Besides, it's not like either she or Clara had known Eleri for long... Perhaps Sioned was justified in having doubts.

Sioned, who was now worrying her bottom lip between her teeth, looked back and forth between Clara and Charles. As much as she wanted to, Clara couldn't give her the reassurance she was looking for. The blonde gave a small, helpless shrug, which Charles caught out of the corner of his eye.

He turned to Clara, brown eyes full of compassion, and placed a hand on her shoulder. It must have pulled on his stitches, to have his arms each extended like that, but Charles still managed it. He had placed the cup of tea on the ground by his leg, kindly ignoring his own pain and its potential relief in favour of comforting his hosts. Clara was filled with admiration, and suddenly grew to resent Eleri and her aloof treatment of an injured man.

"Ah, you know what, girls? My home is not very far away, I was headed there when I was attacked," Charles said. "Why don't we all head there together, and you can rest awhile indoors and rework your plan?"

Sioned instantly relaxed at this proposal. She put her hand over Charles' where it rested on her knee and gave him a smile that could rival the sun. After a brief moment, she flipped his hand upwards and put the teacup in it again.

"That's a great idea! Here, drink up so you can be as comfortable as possible while we walk. We'll pack up, and we can go as soon as you're ready."

Sioned made to stand, ready to start the clean up. Clara, too, thought this was a wonderful plan, as it would mean they wouldn't have to spend all day in the rain and the next night in damp clothes and blankets.

"Excuse me. I didn't agree to this." Eleri's voice was cold.

Sioned paused mid-movement, ending up in a strange half crouch. She looked over her shoulder with a confused frown.

"Well, it's not like you're the boss of us; we're equals," Sioned explained, as if talking to a child. "We don't need your permission to go anywhere. And you can't tell me you'd rather stay in the rain all day than go to Charles' house."

"I'd rather stay in the rain all day than go to Charles' house," Eleri said. Her tone was even, but it held an undercurrent of annoyance. "I don't know him; I don't like strangers. And I don't like when plans change unexpectedly."

"So what? You'd stubbornly choose to soak yourself instead of meeting someone new? That's the dumbest thing I've ever heard," Clara exclaimed.

Eleri glowered, and, pettily, Clara was glad to have broken her carefully-curated mask of indifference. It didn't help that the rain had fully soaked Eleri by this point, giving her the appearance of a soggy kitten.

"I can meet new people. I agreed to travel with you, and I know when I need to accept outside help. I am just also on a schedule, and don't want an unnecessary delay. We can take Charles home, but not stay with him." Then, Eleri shrugged. "He seems much better than last night, anyway."

"You're frigid." Sioned sounded more disappointed than Clara had ever heard. "We can take Charles home, and it sounds like he knows the way to Gryphon's Keep, too. We don't need you, or your schedule."

Clara made a noise of agreement and Charles lit up. He placed a hand on his heart, looking like he had just been given the world. It made a warm feeling take hold in Clara's chest, which was a soothing balm against the chill of the rain that now invaded her body.

"Sioned, Clara, you ladies have been so good to me. Of course I would be willing to accompany you to the Keep. After all, you have saved my life. My home, my time, it is all yours."

Charles took a sip of his tea and immediately choked on it, sputtering and dribbling some of the drink down his chin. Sioned handed him a kerchief, which he used to dab at his face and chest. Clara rubbed soothing circles on his back, though she was careful not to disturb the wrapped bandages.

"What was that? Ugh, that was vile," Charles exclaimed through coughs.

"What did you give him? He's injured!" Sioned rounded on Eleri, her fists balled up at her sides.

"It's *willow bark*," Eleri protested, rolling her eyes. "It always tastes bitter. That's why I added the mint."

Sioned stood, the top of her head brushing against the canvas shelter and sending a gout of water rushing over the edge. It splashed near Eleri and soaked her left boot completely. While she was inspecting the extent of the damage, twisting her foot to and fro and frowning at what she saw, Sioned grew more irritable and aggressive.

"Stop ignoring me! Staring down at your boot like it's the most important thing!" Sioned shouted. "There's an injured man here, and you're treating him with such contempt."

Eleri gave Sioned a look of pure exasperation.

"I have every right to be suspicious of a man who claims the Forest of Yor is too dangerous for me to travel in, but lives there himself and suggests we stay there."

Clara shuffled closer to both Charles and Sioned during this time. She wrapped one hand around Sioned's wrist, hoping that the other woman would interpret it as a sign of support. Clara also made sure that none of the water that spilled off their shelter had fallen on Charles. It wouldn't do to let his bandages get soaked. When she bent over to check the fabric, the pressure in her head spiked painfully.

Clara sat back with a groan and rubbed at her temple with her free hand. The pain stayed even after she sat up, and was now coupled with a foggy, lightheaded feeling. Charles gave her a sympathetic grin, holding out his cup.

"Maybe you need this more than me, if you can stomach the taste," he laughed.

Clara felt her affection for him swell but didn't take the cup. Her headache was nothing compared to being attacked by some kind of animal. Sioned twisted her hand in Clara's grip to hold hands properly and spared a brief glance over her shoulder at Clara.

"Look! Clara isn't feeling well, either. And neither am I; it must be all this damp air. We should rest in Charles' cottage until we all recover." Then Sioned's face twisted into a malicious sneer, one that looked incredibly foreign on her face. "If you can care about other people more than your stupid schedule, that is."

Eleri looked taken aback for a moment and recoiled minutely from Sioned's strange vitriol. She looked between the three of them with confusion, her face suddenly appeared impossibly young. This vulnerability didn't deter Sioned in the slightest.

"This is probably why your mom doesn't want you, and your dad didn't stick around to see you be born! They knew you wouldn't be worth it!" Sioned sucked in a great, heaving breath, stumbled dizzily, and like Clara, raised a hand to her temple. She recovered quickly, however, and continued shouting at Eleri. "Even when a kind, injured man offers you help, you are so suspicious of him for no reason."

"Are you feeling it, too?" Eleri asked softly. "The headache, the cottony feeling when you think, tiredness..."

This gentle questioning did not soothe Sioned in the slightest. Rather, it only irritated her more.

"If you know our symptoms, I'm guessing that means you're sick, too! Why are you so stubborn about accepting help? Goddesses above, you are so annoying."

Eleri's face became carefully blank. Clara distantly remembered that that seemed to be a defence mechanism with her, but it was hard to remember why she cared.

"I see what's going on here," Eleri said, but it was almost inaudible over the sounds of the rain and the pounding in Clara's head.

Sioned's hand was trembling in her own, and Clara felt more than a little nauseous after Sioned's animated yelling had jerked her body around. Clara started to sway dangerously and pitched forward. She would have hit the ground face-first had Charles not grabbed her and hauled her upright again.

Sioned spun around and all but collapsed at Clara's side. Her face was ashen and her eyes glassy, and Clara thought the other woman looked like she was about to be sick. They squeezed the other's hands at the same time, then gave matching watery smiles as they tried to comfort each other in the same way. Charles' brown eyes were full of concern as he stared at her, while supporting her whole upper body with his arms. Clara only had a second to appreciate the tenderness he showed her.

In the few seconds it had taken for all of this to transpire, Eleri had crossed the clearing and forced herself back under the canvas shelter. She stood there, dripping wet but straight and proud with an expression of determined fury on her face. It was almost too much for Clara to process in her tired and confused state, but her brain sparked to life at the sight of Eleri's sword pressed firmly into the skin of Charles' neck.

Chapter Thirteen

The cottony feeling in her head, along with the searing headache, dulled Sioned's reaction time. She blinked sleepily at the sight of Eleri's blade against Charles' neck, and though she could distantly feel some kind of upset, it was hard to understand it through the brain fog. Only when Clara made a noise of distress did Sioned find enough willpower to make a move.

Since Sioned had been standing by the edge of the shelter, on the left-hand side, she was now the closest to Eleri. She lurched to her feet and made a grab for Eleri's sword hand.

Eleri, however, was expecting this. Without looking away from Charles, she took hold of Sioned's wrist and twisted her arm back against her chest. Sioned cried out in alarm, which drew a confused, pained sound from Clara. Using her grip as leverage, Eleri forced Sioned into a kneeling position, despite the height difference and the odd angle.

"Don't start," Eleri warned, still holding Sioned's wrist.

"Now, what's all this, then?" Charles asked soothingly. Clara was still wrapped in his arms, and he drew her closer to lie against his chest. "You poor girls, having to travel with someone as strange and unstable as Miss Eleri... I'll keep you safe from now on."

Eleri flipped her wrist, so the sharpened edge of her sword left a thin, shallow line of red along his neck. He had to angle his head away to keep the pressure off, but kept his eyes, so full of rage, trained on Eleri's.

"Let them go," Eleri said, her voice even but filled with restrained anger.

Something dark and gleeful sparkled in Charles' eyes. The rage was still there, but now it was held back by a sense of returned control. He barked out an ugly laugh, which showed off a mouth full of ragged fangs.

"You really are a pathetic, disgusting, failure of a girl. Are you mad that your friends finally realised you're not worth it? Jealous they found someone better?"

Eleri's face twisted in confusion, and she shook her head minutely. Her grip never wavered on either her sword or Sioned. The head shake seemed to have cleared her mind again, as Eleri refocused on Charles, looking more determined than ever.

Clara made another distressed sound in Charles' arms, which was echoed by Sioned. Charles shushed them, as one would a baby. When he returned his attention to Eleri, she wore a glittering, sharp smile. She looked more like a triumphant predator than anything else.

"Attacking an injured man? That's so cruel." Charles put on a woe-begotten voice, but it rang hollow in Eleri's ears.

"Not exactly injured anymore, are you, shapeshifter?" Eleri nodded her chin at Charles' neck, where the thin cut had already disappeared.

"Oh, but my poor shoulder and chest hurt! Don't you feel any pity?" Charles asked with a whine, pushing out his bottom lip in a pout.

"You're not hurt there either, anymore." Eleri rolled her eyes. "If you can both lift and have Clara, who is taller than you, lean on your bad side, then those nasty gouges must be gone. Besides, why else would Sioned and Clara be so affected if you weren't feeding on them?"

When Charles understood that the game was over, he dropped all pretenses. He snarled, double rows of sharp teeth on full display, and the pupil of his brown eyes dilated until it turned them fully black. His grip on Clara tightened and he dug newly-revealed claws into her arm. Clara, who still lay half-asleep and confused in Charles' arms, flinched, then moaned in pain.

Sioned, with her arm still pinned in Eleri's grip, blinked blearily at the noise. It seemed to awaken something in her, as her eyes were clearer and more focused after. She struggled a moment against

Eleri but quickly exhausted herself and slumped down, held up only by Eleri's arm.

Not taking her eyes off Charles, or her blade, Eleri slowly crouched down and allowed Sioned to lie on the forest floor. She looked miserable and pained, more so than even Charles had looked at the height of his injuries, and stayed put. The only movement was the rise and fall of Sioned's chest and her eyes as they tracked Eleri's actions.

As soon as her hand was free, Eleri slid around Charles. It happened in a flash, Eleri moving as quickly and as gracefully as possible. She now knelt behind him, with her sword pressed more securely against his neck. When Charles noticed his now more vulnerable position, he froze, feeling Eleri's measured breath against his ear. This moment of shock was just enough for Eleri to grab hold of Clara's collar and yank her from Charles' grasp. The blonde landed rather harshly on her side nearby and coughed lightly but was otherwise okay.

"A failure *and* violent? I feel so bad for your friends... You've thrown them both to the ground like garbage."

Eleri laughed, clear and cold. Her left hand came down on Charles' shoulder with an iron grip; her right remained steady and held the sword straight.

"Oh, Charles... I grew up with a mother that wanted me dead. There is nothing you can say to me that will hurt me in the way you want."

Eleri's free hand came up to pat Charles' cheek condescendingly, then returned to his shoulder.

"Now. I think it's time you and I go for a little walk. I just wanted to make sure Sioned and Clara were safe—"

Eleri gasped as she suddenly tipped to the side, bringing Charles down with her by his neck. Clara had, unseen by either Eleri or Charles, grabbed a fistful of Eleri's tunic and yanked it. This new position had Charles laying on top of Eleri, and he squirmed around to face her. His face was victorious as he stared down at the girl beneath him. Eleri struggled, but with the leverage he had, Charles was able to pin one of her hands under each knee. Charles unhooked Clara's unresistant fingers from Eleri's tunic and all but tossed Eleri's sword aside. Eleri couldn't see where it went but heard the rustle of foliage to the right side of her.

"Mmmmm, a fresh meal." Charles bent down to sniff at Eleri's neck. "You've some real *zing* in you, too. Not sure what it is, but I bet it'll keep me full for a long time."

Eleri continued to try to throw Charles off her. It made no difference. A strangle ripple effect passed over Charles' skin, like an air pocket was travelling the length of his body. After it had passed, Eleri could see that his muscles were bigger, and she felt the increased weight on her abdomen where Charles sat. At this, Eleri stopped moving. Charles looked down in surprise, his face making a comical 'O' with his mouth.

"Giving up already, are you? Hope that doesn't affect your flavour; the other two were a little too... common for my liking."

Charles then laughed at the obstinate look that was still on Eleri's face. Her brow was furrowed, and her lips were set in a grim line, but her eyes were alive with shimmering rage. However, when Charles tilted her chin up to bare her neck, there was no resistance.

"Love the anger, but it's nice to see you've realised there is nothing you can do. I'm quite full from your friends, so I think I'll just drain you enough to keep you quiet, then take all three of you back to my house... How's that for disrupting your schedule?"

Charles, still bent over Eleri's supine form, grazed his nose along Eleri's neck. She could feel him grin and was barely able to repress her shudder of disgust. Charles was still gloating, but Eleri tuned him out, staring straight ahead at the underside of the canvas shelter, enduring. Clara moaned, and Charles shifted to look over at her.

That was a mistake. He reared back and howled in pain, one hand coming to clamp tightly to his neck, which was now gushing blood.

As soon as Charles began to shift his weight, Eleri started to yank on her hands where they were trapped by his knees. Once they were free, Eleri was quick to slide out from between his legs.

Collecting himself, Charles refocused on the girl crouched in front of him. Eleri's lower jaw and her bared teeth were stained bright red with Charles' blood. She even needed a moment to spit a piece of flesh out of her mouth, though she kept her eyes trained on Charles' face the entire time. Her shoulders were heaving with every breath she took; she looked wild and fierce.

"You bit me! Were you trying to tear my throat out like a rabid dog?" Charles lunged for Eleri again, but she rolled out of the way. "You little good-for-nothing wretch!"

They continued in this pattern, Charles doing his best to leap at Eleri, with her evading each attempt. His movements were hampered by the hand he still had pressed to his bleeding neck, but Eleri was on the defensive with no way to counter his attacks besides dodging. Charles developed a manic grin as they performed this strange little routine.

"What's your plan now, little miss Eleri? You have nowhere to go, nobody is coming to save you. And now, you've just made me mad."

Eleri ignored this, making another desperate roll to the left. She ended up on her bottom, back against a sturdy tree. Her arms were splayed to either side, leaving her torso open to attack. There were bushes to the left and to the right of her, and she could see the thorns growing on their stems. She had barely a second to herself before Charles was looming over her again.

"Backed yourself into quite a corner, now, didn't you? Should have paid better attention to what you were doing," Charles laughed.

He took his hand from his neck, allowing it to bleed freely though the blood was already clotting. With both arms, he reached for Eleri at a leisurely pace. He was clearly enjoying watching her squirm, her hands scrabbling at the bushes and dirt around her.

Charles kept his eyes trained on Eleri's face, riveting by the look of fear on it. The first brush of his hands on her shoulders was tender, paternalistic, then Charles clamped down, his claws biting into the flesh through Eleri's clothes.

Watching Eleri's face gave Charles a split-second warning. The wide-eyed look melted off, replaced with a calm confidence. Before Charles could even process this, there was a pain in his abdomen. It felt like he had been punched, and he wanted to gloat about desperate, last-minute actions, when he felt something warm and wet trickle down his front.

"Perhaps it was you who should have been paying more attention," Eleri chirped.

Everything in Charles' brain had been reduced to the point of pain in his stomach. Eleri's words sounded distant and distorted to his ears. There was a sharp stabbing feeling that sent his pain levels spiking up, which finally spurned him into action. He looked down and saw that Eleri had driven her sword straight into his gut.

The sharp feeling returned. Since he was looking down, this time Charles could see it was caused by Eleri slowly pressing her sword further into his body, as she was hampered by the lack of leverage her position offered. With a final shove, her blade made it all the way through his torso. Immediately, Eleri pulled her sword free, leaving Charles without its support.

Two weak spurts of blood, one from Charles' neck, and one from the newly-made wound in his abdomen, splashed out onto Eleri. She knocked his hands from her shoulders and stood, watching impassively as Charles slumped to the forest floor.

Clara, who had been drained the most by Charles, still lay on the ground under their shelter. She was sprawled out, facing away, with her arm still outstretched from when she had reached for Eleri. Clara was pale and shivering, but she was breathing steadily now, and was likely out of danger. Sioned had fared a little better. She propped herself up by the elbows, staring at Eleri with wide eyes and trembling lips. Sioned hadn't moved much since Eleri laid her down, just twisted her body to be able to watch the fight, which resulted in her legs being out from under the shelter.

Dripping with rain and blood, Eleri made her way over to Sioned. Her steps were light, soft, and slow, and she kept her hands raised to chest level, palms out in a display of gentle submission, but Sioned still flinched at Eleri's approach. Eleri winced in response, eyes downcast, but kept coming closer.

Sioned opened her mouth and made a sound that might have been a 'no' had she been stronger. Eleri winced again but took Sioned by the arms as gently as she could.

"I know. I know. I'm sorry," Eleri soothed, bringing Sioned fully under the shelter.

The sight of red handprints on Sioned's pretty yellow sleeves made Eleri nauseous. She tried her best to wipe her hands clean on her muddy wet tunic. When she deemed them as good as they were going to get, Eleri unpacked Sioned's blanket from her bag and tucked the other girl in. She did the same for Clara, then stepped out from under the shelter.

It was raining in earnest now. Unlike the gentle drizzle it had started as, which took time to fully dampen Eleri's hair, this downpour would have soaked her instantly. As it was, she stood for a moment, face tilted to the sky, letting the water run down her body in rivulets.

Eleri heaved a great sigh, straightened her shoulders, and went back to where Charles' body lay. She rolled him onto his back and felt for a pulse. When she felt nothing, she rounded the body to where the feet were. Eleri cast a look back at Sioned and Clara, who were watching and sleeping respectively, and picked up Charles' feet. She held one in each hand, rested the body's ankles on her hips, and dragged the corpse into the woods.

Ideally, the three women would leave the area, but with Sioned and Clara so weakened it wasn't possible. Eleri simply had to hope that moving the body and the heavy rain would do enough to dull the smell of blood and keep the scavengers away from them.

Chapter Fourteen

Sioned could not tell how long it took for Eleri to return to their campsite. She was curled up under her blanket, listening to the pounding of the rain on the canvas above her and staring rather blankly at the forest around her. There was a damp chill in the air that her single cover couldn't keep out. Sioned shivered.

Summoning all her strength, Sioned turned over and shuffled towards Clara. The blonde was also shivering under her blanket but remained asleep. There was a pinched, pained expression on Clara's face, which looked slightly green. Sioned tucked herself into the curve of Clara's body, curling up with her head under the older woman's chin, and did her best to arrange the blankets over both of them. It helped to keep out the cold, but all the effort left Sioned feeling muzzily, trembling in every limb.

Sioned was drifting between wakefulness and unconsciousness when a hand on her shoulder startled her. Her body twitched violently at the shock, but she had no energy for anything else.

"My apologies. I didn't mean to startle you," Eleri said, stiffly. "I have some of your things, if you'd like them."

There were the sounds of movement and fabric being shuffled from behind her, but Sioned heard it only distantly. It was not like Eleri was standing far away, more like the world had become muted. Sioned couldn't help the thin, reedy whine that fell from her lips as she drew this conclusion. It was no wonder she hadn't heard Eleri's return, but the dimming of her senses left Sioned feeling vulnerable.

Clara seemed to huddle closer in response to Sioned's distress. At the same time, warmth enveloped them both as Eleri straightened and retucked the blankets already in place and layered more on top. She also rounded the sick pair and placed pillows by their heads. Eleri crouched down and showed Sioned her silk sleeping bonnet, but left it on the pillow as well, seemingly unwilling to touch either woman. Sioned eyed them for a moment but couldn't summon the energy to reach for either the pillow or the bonnet. Instead, she closed her weary eyes and drifted, one part secure in the arms of Clara, the other wondering what the bloodstained Eleri was doing, unseen.

This drifting continued, though for how long Sioned could not say. For the most part, she listened to the sound of her and Clara breathing. Sometimes snatches of Eleri singing permeated her tired brain, probably as the girl moved about the campsite, though Sioned couldn't imagine what Eleri was doing. The deep, dark colour of the clouds in the sky removed any hope of using the sun to estimate time.

Clara first started to move by shuffling closer to Sioned. Her arms, which had laid limp at her sides, came up to wrap around Sioned, and the blonde nuzzled her face against the top of Sioned's head. She hummed low in her throat, a rich and gravelly sound that sent a wave of contentment from the top of Sioned's head down to the tips of her toes. Clara's breaths were still those of someone in deep sleep, so Sioned buried her face against her chest, determined to enjoy these last few moments before she had to face the waking world.

Consciousness must have returned slowly, but soon enough Clara shifted enough to look Sioned in the face, her eyes still glazed. She smiled sleepily down at Sioned, but then bolted upright in terror, looking around the camp wildly. This proved to be too much of a strain, however; and Clara doubled up, clutching her stomach and looked very green again. A light sheen of sweat covered her forehead, and she panted raggedly.

Sioned raised herself up on her elbow and used her other arm to rub comforting circles on Clara's back. It only lasted a moment, as she soon felt her arm shaking with the strain of supporting her body. Before she could collapse, Sioned gently tugged Clara to lay back down, and the two of them curled back up under the blankets together, shaking minutely.

"I have something to settle your stomachs, since you're both awake now." Eleri spoke at a normal volume, but her voice sounded booming. Both Clara and Sioned winced.

Sioned managed to roll over enough to look for Eleri, fighting against her own heavy body and the protective arm of Clara wrapped around her middle. There Eleri stood, face and hands clean of blood, holding a cup of something steaming in each hand. Sioned stared, unsure of what to do or say, but Clara took the need to choose away.

"What happened?" she groaned. Now that her arms were empty, she rolled onto her back and threw an arm over her eyes.

"A shapeshifter. One who feeds on your energy to live," Eleri explained. She lowered herself to sit on her knees next to Sioned, then added thoughtfully, "I think he was genuinely injured at first, and needed sustenance to heal, but then couldn't stop himself from gorging on us."

"How do you know he was... that?" Clara's energy was clearly spent. She had started out strongly, but her voice weakened as she spoke, and she used a vague hand gesture to convey the rest of her thought.

"You were both acting so strangely, and by the end he was hauling you around like you weighed nothing, even though he was supposed to be injured. Obviously, something healed him, and if not magic, then it had to be our own life forces."

Eleri shrugged, rather blasé about the whole thing. Sioned was about to get on her case about it, but she noticed the deep, dark circles under Eleri's eyes and the slumped shoulders instead of her usual good posture. Eleri noticed her staring, and managed a weak smile, holding out the cups in her hands.

"It's ginger tea. It will help and taste good as well. I promise."

Sioned didn't move. Clara grumbled, but managed to find a position that was upright enough to drink something, but not so much that it triggered her nausea. She gratefully took the tea from

Eleri and sipped at it with closed eyes and a hum of contentment. Still, Sioned watched Eleri.

"You killed him."

The simple fact, now spoken, drained Eleri of what was left of her energy. Behind Sioned, Clara spluttered into her tea, demanding clarifications, but Sioned could not bring herself to answer.

"I did." Eleri all but whispered. "I didn't plan to; I was going to let him go. But I promised you I'd keep you safe."

With this confession, Sioned slumped down further into her blankets. She didn't know what to think. Now, she knew that Eleri's talks of protection were more than empty words, but the figure in front of her looked so different from the fighter from before. Eleri sat there, making herself as small as possible. She was still soaked, her long hair plastered to her back, and the mid-cheek length bit of fringe clung tightly to the left side of her face. The ribbons tied on either side of her face were limp and lopsided, adding to her sad state. Eleri looked like a half-drowned kitten, all wide-eyed misery.

"What are you two talking about?" Clara moaned.

Eleri was still folded in on herself, but she shifted enough to put her focus on Clara. The blue of the eye not hidden by her hair almost glowed.

"Charles was killing us. He wanted to keep us and feed off us for as long as possible. I tried to get him to release his hold and just go, but he refused. So I put my sword through his stomach and killed him." Eleri's voice was even and did not waver. "My only regrets are letting it go on as long as it did, and frightening Sioned."

Clara laughed, a sound that was only slightly strained. "You're absolutely tiny. You probably don't weigh half as much as me now when you're soaking wet. How scary can you be?"

"She tried to take his throat out with her teeth."

"I had no plans to die today."

Sioned and Eleri stared at each other for a moment. The rage Sioned had been feeling earlier flared up again at the sight of Eleri's determinedly neutral expression, but she couldn't quite remember the cause of it. Sioned raised a hand to rub at her temple, more than done with the pain and clouded thinking. Eleri tried, yet again, to hand her the remaining cup of tea.

"Please. It will help."

"It does, Sioned," Clara added, who had perked up significantly during the conversation.

Sioned reluctantly took the tea and sipped only the smallest amount. The warmth that flooded through her, both physically and otherwise, was a balm to her aches and pains. She could admit that much.

"I felt... so angry," she said, mostly to herself.

Clara must have heard because she placed a warm hand on Sioned's shoulder. Eleri somehow managed to shrug, despite her shoulders already being tucked up by her ears. She fiddled with her rings for a while, then took a deep breath, letting it out slowly.

"The way they feed... is by bringing the most applicable emotion to the surface and taking your energy that way. It's supposed to help bring the prey closer to them, by taking the shape of a hurt child or sick elderly lady... I suppose Charles had to make do with what we felt about him in that form."

A new kind of nausea, unrelated to the deep exhaustion, settled low in Sioned's stomach. She could also feel the change in Clara's demeanour behind her, despite not looking. It was a strange, distant kind of devastation, knowing that her innermost thoughts had been dragged to the surface and feasted upon by a stranger, but not having enough energy to truly parse what that meant. Unsure of what else to do, Sioned sipped her tea.

"Why weren't you affected, Eleri? You sort of drifted off to do your own thing..."

As soon as Clara asked that, Sioned made the connection to the last minutes of Charles' life, and the things he said to Eleri. A part of her, more nosey than plain curious, desperately wanted to know more, as Eleri had mentioned difficulties with her mother and nothing about her father. Another part worried that Eleri explaining would break the seal, and Sioned herself would be forced to talk about her experience.

Eleri managed a brittle smile. Sioned held her breath, eager and terrified to hear what she would say next.

"I suppose you were too far gone to hear... I was born to a mother who never wanted a daughter, and to a father who was dead long before I came into this world."

"Shouldn't parents care more about having a child than what they are? My parents never cared if they had sons or daughters, just someone to love." Sioned frowned.

Clara snorted derisively. Sioned twisted to see her and, after a moment of dizziness, saw a look of great pain on her face. Her green eyes were haunted by something, and it made Sioned wonder why Clara had been so keen on Charles.

"Some people only want a certain kind of kid, and goddesses help you if you don't fit the mould, right, Eleri?" Clara gave a half-hearted chuckle, trying to make light of the situation.

"I was never meant to be a child, just a means to an end," Eleri said, completely void of emotion. "Being a girl made me replaceable in the line of succession, so my mother would rather have gotten rid of me and tried again for a son."

Sioned looked between the two of them, feeling quite alien in this conversation. The idea of an unwanted child had never crossed her mind before now.

"I feel awful now, wanting to complain about my parents being *too* loving." Sioned tried for a joking tone, but it fell flat.

Her false smile curdled and slid off her face. Neither Clara or Eleri reacted, and Sioned floundered for a moment. The implications of what Eleri said hit her.

"Gotten rid of? That's... You can't mean that, now or when you said it to Charles," Sioned all but pleaded.

"I was disowned, you know," Clara said. "Too different, I couldn't be the son they wanted either. Even when I changed and my magic quickened, they couldn't see being *Clara* instead of their precious son was the right choice for me. Sometimes parents will do what they can to remove what they see as a blight on the family. Not sure how your mother planned to 'try again' with your dad being dead and all, though."

Sioned turned and pulled Clara into her arms. She wanted to embrace Eleri as well, but the image of her bloodied face was still fresh in her mind. Clara made a noise of surprise when Sioned nuzzled into her chest, but brought her hand to the back of Sioned's head. She gently rubbed the rows of intricate braids, doing her best to provide comfort without ruining the hairstyle.

"I wasn't... conceived naturally. I was only born through the use of magic," Eleri began haltingly.

"There's no shame in that; plenty of couples turn to fertility rites when they struggle," Clara interrupted. Even with her face hidden, Sioned could feel the tension in the air.

"My father was long dead before I was born. Long dead before my grandfather was born," Eleri added, thoughtfully. "My mother and her conspirators used a spell to bring me forth into this world; it used the Apoginos flower. When I was born, a disappointment from the first breath, they planned to raise me for the ten years it took for the flower to bloom again. Then they would use my blood in the same rite and try for a boy. A son who would be king, or at least wield his father's sword. Someone easier to manipulate into political or martial power."

"Goddesses above..." Sioned breathed into Clara's shirt.

Clara said nothing, but she had gotten progressively more tense as Eleri had spoken, though whether she was more unnerved by Eleri's words, or her clipped, clinical tone, Sioned couldn't tell.

"Well," Eleri broke the silence. There was a rustle of clothing, which Sioned assumed was Eleri getting to her feet. "This has been an all-around terrible experience. Truly, though, I don't blame you. I am going to go climb a tree and have a good cry in it. Don't follow me."

Sioned peeled her face away from Clara just enough to watch Eleri walk stiffly into the woods. She paused just at the edge of being visible and turned back to point at them.

"Drink your tea. It will help."

Then she was obscured from sight by the trees. Sioned and Clara looked at each other, unsure of what to say. They separated, a little awkwardly, and each reclaimed their cups of tea from where they sat.

The steam was still billowing from each cup. Sioned thought nothing of it, just enjoying the almost scalding drink, but Clara inspected it closely.

"I wonder..." she trailed off, then continued at Sioned's questioning look. "The tea is still piping hot. Despite how long we've been talking, and the cold weather... And however long before we woke up that Eleri made it..."

Clara looked thoughtful, poking a finger into her tea. She had to pull it out swiftly and shake it around in the air to cool it off and remove the sting of its heat. Clara passed the arm that had her wand strapped under her sleeve over the cup, muttering a quick spell.

"Her tea always stays hot; her pack is deeper than it should be... but there are no obvious enchantments on either. It makes me think..." Clara's voice grew distant.

Sioned wordlessly prompted her again, and Clara shook her head slowly, as if coming out of a dream.

"I couldn't use my magic until I was true to myself, as a woman. I wonder if there isn't something in Eleri, too, but there's something holding her back."

Chapter Fifteen

Their tea did not cool. Sioned and Clara kept sipping at it, drinking slowly to not upset their stomachs. The ginger in it helped, and soon most of the pain and dizziness had passed, though they both still felt very weak. They mostly sat or laid in their bedrolls, resting and talking. The rest of the afternoon passed like this, with Sioned and Clara cocooned together for warmth and company.

Eleri did not reappear until their usual dinner time. Her footsteps were so quiet that the others did not hear her approach and were startled to see her standing before them. Eleri was just as soaked as before, but now her hair was dishevelled in a way that suggested she had been running her hands through it, and her blue eyes were rimmed with red.

They stared at each other quietly for a moment, then Eleri seemed to come back to herself.

"Feeling better, yeah? I can make something for dinner. The two of you should eat something to regain your strength," Eleri said softly, though her voice was congested and a little crackly.

"Are you... alright?" Clara asked hesitantly.

Eleri, who had been rummaging through the cooking supplies, looked up with a startled expression.

"Oh, yes. I had a nice cry and now it's all out of my system," she said, and genuinely sounded cheerier than before. "Now. How does stew sound? I think I have a little bit of preserved chicken left..."

"What? Yes, that's fine," Sioned dismissed. "But dinner isn't really the most important thing at the moment."

Eleri didn't respond. She started dinner preparations, focusing on the task at hand with a ferocity that was unnecessary for warming chicken and cutting vegetables. Clara shifted to lean over Sioned and place her hand on Eleri's shoulder. Eleri stiffened, but otherwise didn't acknowledge it.

"Eleri…"

Eleri turned suddenly, loose brown waves flying wildly around her head. Clara pulled her hand away, shocked.

"I am not willing to discuss my mother anymore, thank you very much," Eleri said primly. "I understand it is an unusual situation, which invites curiosity, but it is also very unpleasant to reminisce on."

Eleri's voice may have been formal and even keeled, but there was a haunted look in her eyes that belied the emotional toll. For a moment, it looked like she would cry again, but she blinked back the tears to stare Clara and Sioned down.

Sioned held up her hands in surrender. At the same time, Clara set each teacup down in front of Eleri, allowing them to thud dramatically on the forest floor.

"These are still warm to the touch."

This snapped Eleri out of her tears, and she made a face of pure confusion. She shrugged, then raised her hands in a kind of *what-can-I-say* gesture.

"Alright. They're still warm. Would you like another cup of tea with dinner?" Eleri asked, though her tone made it clear she was just humouring Clara.

"I—yes, sure. That would be nice. Can I watch you make it?"

At Clara's words, Eleri's mouth did a little twist, almost like she was trying not to laugh. She reached behind herself to grab her pack and brought it around to sit in her lap.

"If you'd like to, I suppose," she acquiesced.

Eleri pulled out a small tin from her bag, similar in size and shape to what she usually had in the mornings. She opened it and held it out for Clara—and Sioned when she leaned in—to smell. It had a strong gingery aroma, just like the tea they'd had.

Clara watched Eleri go through the motions of making tea like a hawk. All the while, Eleri was fighting a smile, apparently very amused by it all. She even allowed Clara to inspect her water-skin and tea making utensils, showing them off with dramatic hand flourishes.

Clara didn't press Eleri to take it more seriously. For one thing, it was nice to see her smile again, despite the evidence of tears still on her freckled cheeks. It also seemed needlessly cruel to get Eleri's hopes up without any solid evidence, given that Clara knew her lack of magic was a sore spot.

When Eleri finished making the teas, one for each of them, she sat back with a smile poorly hidden behind her own cup.

"Did that illuminate you? Finding out my secret to making tea?" she teased.

Clara frowned at her own cup. She hadn't, actually. All she saw was ordinary ingredients being used in an ordinary way.

"Is this the same way you made it earlier?" Clara asked.

"It tastes the same," Sioned offered.

"You know that's not what I meant."

Eleri was frowning now, too. She put her cup down and looked shrewdly between Sioned and Clara.

"What is so important about my tea?" she asked, then a look of hesitation crossed Eleri's face. "Is this about... earlier? Do you not trust me?"

"No!" Sioned shouted, then looked horrified when Eleri reared back in shocked dismay. "I mean, no, that's not it. It's just..."

Sioned trailed off helplessly, looking to Clara for help. Clara gave her shoulder a tender and comforting squeeze, then reached forward to hold both of Eleri's hands in her own.

"Eleri, do you know it's weird for tea to stay hot for hours on end?" Clara asked gently.

With her head tilted to allow the long part of her fringe to hide half her face, Eleri's expression was unreadable. A sense of unhappy confusion poured off her in waves, and Eleri seemed lost in thought. Clara tugged lightly on their conjoined hands, trying to recapture Eleri's attention.

"I... really have no idea what you're talking about," Eleri began hesitantly. "I know I was... put together wrong somehow, but I—"

"Oh! No, that's not what we're talking about!" Sioned exclaimed, cutting Eleri off. She dived forward to wrap Eleri in her arms, clearly defaulting back into her big sister patterns at the sight of Eleri's tremulous bottom lip.

Clara had to stifle a laugh. The pair of them were awkwardly smushed together, as Sioned had leaned quite far forward to be able to grab Eleri. This meant that Eleri's full cheek was pressed up against Sioned's shoulder in a way that squished it strangely.

"I've checked it, just like I did your bag. Neither your tea nor your bag show signs of any known enchantment that would explain their oddities, but..." Here Clara paused for a moment, unsure of how or if to continue. "Well. I think you're doing instinctual magic."

Eleri scoffed. It didn't have much bite, seeing as she was still wound tightly in Sioned's embrace.

"I attempted the Trials, multiple times. If there was a drop of magic in my veins, they'd have found it. Besides, I've never had the usual instinctual magic experiences, like knocking things over without touching them, or windstorms."

"I don't know, Eleri," Sioned said, looking thoughtful. "The wind was blowing pretty hard when you were challenging Charles."

"Sioned, there was a thunderstorm," Eleri said in disbelief.

"Just... think about it," Clara told her. "I didn't come into my magic until I transitioned. If you think you might be 'put together wrong' then you might be blocking yourself."

The emotions that flickered across Eleri's face were almost too rapid to read. Hope, surprise, anger, disbelief, happiness, and then her expression shuttered and became the carefully neutral mask they had seen time and time again. She had been preparing dinner while they talked, and now slid the final ingredients into the pot and put the lid on it. Eleri wiped her hands on her thighs, dusting the remnants of cooking and the conversation.

"You've given me a lot to think about..." Eleri said, though it was clear her mind was already somewhere else. "Excuse me, but please don't hesitate to ask if you need something."

Eleri drifted off, as far as one could go under their little shelter. She was finally starting to dry off, and though it would be a slow process, at least she was only damp instead of soaked. When she got to the edge of the canvas, she sat down and pulled her little battered notebook from her pack and started idly flipping through it.

Clara leaned in to whisper in Sioned's ear, low enough to not disturb Eleri.

"All that time in the rain and the book isn't wrecked? There is definitely something more to that stupid bag."

Sioned hummed in agreement, shifting back to rest against Clara's warm chest. She didn't do it consciously, but the memory of being wrapped in the other woman's arms still lingered in her mind.

With the rain still pattering against the canvas above them and night settling in around them, it was shaping up to be a lovely evening despite all odds. Clara and Sioned kept quiet, partly due to exhaustion, and simply enjoyed their time together. Soon enough, Eleri rejoined them, saying that dinner was ready.

She served them each half-bowls of stew at first, saying they could have more if their stomach could handle it. Neither Sioned nor Clara was willing to push it, though. When dinner was done, Eleri brought out her bed roll and laid out near the other two.

"We should still be able to reach Gryphon's Keep within the day or so, provided the two of you are recovered enough to walk that far," Eleri told them.

This was somewhat surprising to Clara and Sioned. They stared at Eleri as she shuffled her way under her blankets, open-mouthed.

Sioned recovered first. "Are we really that close?"

"Yes," Eleri shrugged. The Forest of Yor isn't the biggest area, besides, and we've already gotten partway through it."

Eleri leaned back on one hand, the other coming up to tap a slender finger against her chin. She hummed lightly, deep in thought.

"There will likely be other creatures like the shapeshifter as we go further, little things that like to get you psychologically, rather than simply eating you alive. That's what makes the Forest of Yor so dangerous."

"Don't say that so casually!" Clara scolded, swatting lightly at Eleri's shoulder.

Eleri merely giggled and leaned away.

"It sounds terrible! But I am warning you, and I do have some suggestions on how to protect yourself." Then Eleri paused, considering. "Aside from letting me handle it with a sword."

Sioned rolled her bottom lip between her teeth, thinking back on the way she had seen Eleri dispatch Charles. It had been the first time she'd ever seen anything like it, and despite the way Eleri had described her competency with the blade, it had been very unnerving to see her small friend look so deadly.

Eleri clearly noticed this, as her smile dimmed. She did her best to not let it show, but there was also a certain defeated posture to her shoulders. Clara looked between the two, a little lost. It was evident that Clara and Sioned's energy levels were also waning. Clara, who had been targeted more heavily, had started to sway and even nod off. Despite this, she tried her best to stay alert, both to understand the fractures between Sioned and Eleri and to hear Eleri's advice.

"The most important thing is to remember that you cannot trust anything you feel in the Forest of Yor. The only safe place once you step foot there is within Gryphon's Keep and its protective wards," Eleri began, using her hands to make a circular gesture when describing the Keep.

"Is that really good advice?" Sioned asked doubtfully.

"I think so." Eleri shrugged. "I just try to make no emotional choices while I'm there, just focus on getting through as soon as possible."

"Even if you see nothing out of the ordinary?" Sioned asked.

"*Especially* if I see nothing out of the ordinary," Eleri said sagely, nodding her head. "If I see something, it's desperate. Manipulation works best if you don't know it's happening."

This seemed to be an obvious pronouncement, but the gravitas with which Eleri said it prevented Clara from pointing this out. Eleri took her hand away from her face, index finger still extended. The firelight caught on the silver of her ring.

"First thing to do before when dealing with the Forest of Yor is examine what your insecurities are. Personally, my relationship with my mother is one, and so I make it a point to ignore when the forest itself begins to whisper insults to me in her voice."

Clara looked at Sioned in concern and was gratified to see that she looked apprehensive as well, since Eleri was so cavalier. Eleri added a second finger.

"Secondly, any hard feelings between us must wait to be addressed until after we are back in a safe zone. Even if they are natural, any hint of infighting will only draw more danger towards us. We can have it out with each other at the Keep if we want to."

This was met with nods from the other two. Eleri put up a third finger.

"The last bit of advice I have is to have something to hold on to. I suppose that one is more of a recommendation than a must, but I have always felt that I can make my way through the Forest of Yor easier that way."

"Hold on to?" Sioned asked uncertainly.

"Mhm. Usually, I focus on my task, like leading someone through the forest or delivering whatever it is I have. I tell myself, as long as I can do that, I will be alright. It is a temporary goal that helps me resist the pull of despair. Though—" Here Eleri laughed. "I did once guide a man through Yor who told me he just thought about how much he loved his wife the entire time."

This also brought smiles to Sioned and Clara's faces. It was such a sweet image. Eleri finished fussing with her blankets and laid down with a yawn that triggered the other two to do so as well.

"We'll have some time in the morning before we set off, so feel free to ask any questions about the Forest of Yor then. But for now, rest."

And with that, all three women laid down and allowed sleep to claim them.

Chapter Sixteen

The next morning dawned humid and heavy. The moisture in the air from all the rain mixed with the return of the unseasonable heat created an oppressive atmosphere. In spite of the difference in textures, Sioned and Eleri were able to commiserate over the way their curls turned frizzy, while Clara simply mourned the limpness of her thin, straight, blonde locks. Eleri tamed hers with a long dark braid that she twisted into a bun, to keep her thick hair off the nape of her neck. She even found time to complain that it hadn't dried completely over night after the soaking she got in the rain.

It made for an uncomfortable journey. All three of them were sticky with sweat, drained of energy, and consumed by their thoughts about the dangers of the Forest of Yor. Eleri, who had spent the majority of their time travelling humming, if not outright singing to herself, was grim and quiet. There was a red flush high up on the apple of her cheeks and her fringe was damp and plastered to her face. She looked more uncomfortable than she had when standing, dripping wet, in the middle of a thunderstorm.

"I would rather be rained on than sweaty, I mean it," Eleri asserted.

"Your clothes are wet either way," Clara tried to reason with her.

"Sweat and rain are *completely* different sensations," Eleri insisted. "One is sticky and salty and *vile,* and the other is completely natural."

Eleri drew up short, exchanged a disbelieving look with Clara, and started to laugh.

"Er, they're both natural, I know that. Perhaps it's time for a little break?"

Sioned and Clara laughed too, and the three of them found a little shaded area with thicker tree cover to sit under.

"Rain smells better," Eleri continued thoughtfully, after she had had some water.

"Focus," Sioned told her, smiling, and reached over to tap teasingly on Eleri's temple. "You said we'd talk more about the Forest of Yor this morning."

Sioned had spent the morning putting on a cheery affect, but there were still bags under her eyes and a nervousness to her actions. She clearly hadn't fully recovered from her ordeal, or gotten used to the idea of the danger they would soon be in. Both Sioned and Clara, however, had still been too exhausted at breakfast to want to talk about the safety precautions Eleri had mentioned the night before.

Sioned had stuck very close to Clara all morning, sometimes even walking tucked up under Clara's arm. This kept them as close as they could stand to be in the heat, and they only separated when they needed to cool off for a moment. Even now they sat pressed shoulder-to-shoulder, leaning on one another. Eleri had initially assumed it was for balance and support, drained of energy as they were, but now wondered if some of it wasn't partly due to a desire for comfort.

Eleri rolled her shoulders and faced Sioned straight on, her expression calm and serious. There wasn't much else she could think of to say about the forest and its dangers, but she had been told before that she could be too dismissive of peril, and wanted to ensure that Sioned was feeling as comfortable as possible about the future.

"What's on your mind, Sioned?" Eleri asked.

The other woman pursed her lips, looking like she had just eaten something sour. Sioned looked hesitantly between Clara and Eleri, then said, in a hushed, confessional tone:

"I don't think I'll be able to make it through."

Clara immediately started protesting this, but Eleri cut her off with a raised hand. She nodded at Sioned, face impassive, encouraging Sioned to continue.

"I just... was so angry," Sioned said. "I don't know if something like Charles comes after us again, I won't turn on you two, and I couldn't stand it if I did something that truly hurt you."

Her mouth opening and closing without sound, Sioned struggled to continue. She sent a helpless look at Clara, who still looked ready to jump to her defence at a moment's notice. Sioned bit her lip, worrying it between her teeth until the skin gave way and a drop of blood beaded up.

Eleri passed over a handkerchief but said nothing, allowing Sioned time to gather her thoughts. Sioned dabbed at her mouth delicately, then crumpled the fabric in her hands. Her grip was white-knuckled in the tense silence.

"I feel awful bringing it up, especially knowing what I know about your childhoods, and I hate about myself, but when my family feels smothering, it builds up this rage inside of me..."

Clara reached forward to tuck Sioned securely under her arm and pressed her face into the side of Sioned's head, all but kissing the neat, braided rows of hair.

"As if there is a finite amount of pain in this world," Eleri scoffed.

Then she gentled and pulled one of Sioned's hands into both of hers. With a tender smile, Eleri brought Sioned's hand to her mouth in a courtly kiss. Sioned started, and when she met Eleri's gaze, it was full of playful mischief.

"The fact that you worry so much about hurting us shows your true character, Lady Sioned. I have no doubt it will help you resist the pull of any machinations we encounter."

Sioned whimpered at the use of her formal title, a little put out that her attempts at anonymity were for naught. At the same time, Clara reared back in shock, putting distance between her and Sioned unlike what they had seen since the beginning of their journey, face flushing a deep red with embarrassment.

"I, what? Like, *the* Lady Sioned, of the Eastgate family?" Clara manages to choke out.

Sioned nodded miserably, her cheeks also darkening. She took to twisting and untwisting Eleri's handkerchief.

"Well, yes. I hope you can forgive me for lying, even by omission," Sioned implored Clara, looking up at the blonde woman through her lashes. "I just... wanted to enjoy making friends who liked me for me, not my family, you know. It was so *wonderful* to feel like an ordinary person travelling with their friends."

"Terrible time for all of this to come out!" Eleri said, with forced cheer.

Clara and Sioned both frowned at her.

"How long have you known?"

"If it's so terrible to know now, why bring it up?"

Sioned and Clara spoke at the same time. While Sioned was still distraught, Clara was angry and demanding. Eleri shrugged.

"I didn't realise it *wasn't* common knowledge. How many Sioneds who come from big merchant families do you suppose there are?"

When Eleri put it like that, there was little Sioned or Clara could say, though the mutinous look on Clara's face suggested she'd still like to try arguing.

Eleri turned her attention to packing her supplies back up. She stood and dusted her hands off on her legs before looking at her companions.

"Are we ready to crack on?"

There was limited grumbling from the other two, mostly about Eleri's awful timing instead of their continuing walk through the muggy forest.

Unlike the early morning, Clara and Sioned were no longer conjoined at the hip. It was Clara who put the distance there, looking increasingly uncomfortable with Sioned's attempts to press close again, until she put Eleri in between them.

Sioned shrunk in on herself. Eleri knocked their shoulders together in a gesture of comradery, but it only served to make Sioned curl further inwards. Clara walked stiffly on Eleri's other side, looking as uncomfortable as she had when they first met. Clara's green eyes kept darting to the side to look at Sioned, but if Sioned was also looking, Clara would look away quickly with a blush.

Sioned has kept Eleri's handkerchief and twisted it anxiously in her hands as she walked. She, too, kept looking over at Clara, her eyes beseeching the other woman for forgiveness. Every time Clara caught her eye and looked away again, it made Sioned deflate a little more.

All these longing looks from both sides made it so Eleri was constantly being squished and tripped up by the women walking on either side. With every instance, her irritation grew, a deep frown marring her face. Finally, after Eleri tripped over Clara's—or Sioned's, she couldn't tell at this point—foot, she stopped dead in the middle of the path. Sioned and Clara kept walking for a few paces before they noticed Eleri's absence, and then they both turned back to see what the matter was.

There Eleri stood, arms crossed and one foot tapping impatiently. She stared at the two older women with an unamused expression.

"What?" asked Clara.

"I've had more than enough of this," Eleri declared. She reached forward and grabbed a hand from each of them, forcing them to hold hands. "You clearly want to walk beside each other despite it all, so do it. I don't want to be crushed by you two any longer."

Clara flushed a deep, dark red, but didn't say anything or let go of Sioned's hand. Neither of them made any move after that, so Eleri rolled her eyes and surged on ahead, ducking under their conjoined arms.

"Excellent. If that's settled, we can keep going."

Just as Eleri said this, there was a rustle in the leaves to their left. All three of them held their breath, then let out an awkward and relieved chuckle when a small rabbit came bounding out onto the path. They looked between themselves, feeling more than a little silly for being so worried by such a tiny creature.

And then the rabbit was pounced on and devoured by a strange little predator. It had the body of a frog, though it had no legs of any kind. Instead, its plump little body was propelled by a pair of leathery green-black bat wings, stabilised by a whip-thin tail with a wicked-looking stinger at its end. It took the rabbit's neck between its jaw and used one wing to help stabilise itself. In a matter of seconds, the rabbit was gone, skin, bones, and all.

When it had finished eating, the creature gave a baleful croak, wobbling on the tips of its wings as it turned to look at the women. Its beady little eyes squinted at them, full of malice.

The loose grip with which Sioned and Clara had held hands had transformed into a tight grip. They looked frightened as they clung to one another, staring apprehensively at the ravenous little beast.

"*Llamhigyn y Dwr!*" Eleri exclaimed joyfully, her whole face lighting up.

She unclipped her sword sheath from her belt and used the far end to gently prod at the creature. It gave an angry little burble and rolled onto its back to better gnaw on the end of the sheath.

"Excuse me?" Clara asked dubiously, watching as Eleri teased the little thing.

"A Water Leaper," Eleri explained, her focus still mostly on the creature, which had now gotten a good mouthful of her scabbard.

Gripping it partly by the handle of the sword itself, Eleri raised both the scabbard and the Water Leaper into the air, where it hung and squeaked furiously through its mouthful. Sioned giggled weakly.

"They're more dangerous than they look, you know. They mostly like to bite fish right off the line, or sometimes snack on animals that wander too close to the water's edge, but they're not above eating the fisherman himself, if they can manage it."

Sioned startled and withdrew behind Clara, who narrowed her eyes at Eleri.

"Then why have you got it hanging there? Get rid of it!"

Eleri, who had been drawing the end of her scabbard closer and reaching for the Water Leaper, shot Clara a dirty look.

"If it hasn't tried to eat us yet, then it's too full to do so now." She ran a gentle finger along the back of the Water Leaper's spine, then inspected her finger visually and by rubbing it against her thumb. "This little one is quite dry... Must have been out of the water for a while now. Poor thing," Eleri added in a sweet coo directed at the Water Leaper.

"Who cares?" Clara demanded.

"Well, the lake where the Water Leapers live is quite close to Gryphon's Keep, so they're good for getting your bearings, aside from all the good they do for the environment."

Clara still looked doubtful. Her gaze was focused on the Water Leaper, which was still kicking up a fuss as it tried to eat Eleri's scabbard. The little creature's eyes were completely black, but Clara was certain she could see them roving about in their sockets anyway, taking in its entire surroundings. It was hard to tell if it was angrier about not being able to get a bite of the scabbard off, or about being waved around in the air.

"What good could a thing that eats the fishermen do?" Sioned asked, confused and annoyed. "Good people lose their lives to these things."

"Good people lose their lives to wolves, too," Eleri shrugged. "But they still keep the deer and rabbit populations down, which I'm certain the farmers appreciate, even if the royal huntsmen don't always agree."

Eleri swung her sword so that the Water Leaper was hanging near her face and eyed it consideringly. Its body was wracked with tremors of irritation, and it started to squeak and grunt louder and louder as it got closer to Eleri.

"Besides, I think they're rather cute, in a strange way."

Eleri walked off the path into the woods in the direction the Water Leaper had come.

"Come along, then," she called over her shoulder. "There must be a shortcut this way, I know I said to stick to the paths in here, it's too hot for this little fellow to be away from a source of water for long. We'll be alright. Once we've reached its home, we'll be right next to the Keep."

Clara and Sioned looked at each other for a moment, unsure. It was strange to them to dive into the unknown parts of the forest, away from the path, but neither of them knew the area enough to go on without Eleri's guidance. Then, they realised they were still holding hands, and each pulled their own back with lightning speed, looking embarrassed.

"Well! We probably should follow her! Before she gets too far away!" Clara said, a little too loudly.

She also strode into the woods, following Eleri. Her gait was stiff and awkward, like she wanted to get away from Sioned as quickly as possible but wasn't quite sure of the best way to do that.

Sioned was left standing alone in the middle of the path, looking forlorn. She watched the backs of her two companions—Clara rigid and uncomfortable, and Eleri walking with practised ease through the underbrush—then hurried to catch up with them.

Chapter Seventeen

After fighting her way through the branches and brambles, Sioned caught up to Clara and Eleri. They were standing just beyond the tree line, staring at the small lake just ahead. Sioned all but tumbled out of the woods, and Clara grabbed her arm to steady her, then quickly let go again. When Sioned had righted herself and rearranged her clothing, she came to stand beside the other two. The clearing they found themselves in was vaguely hourglass shape, with two mostly circular clearings conjoined in the middle, which was pinched inwards by symmetrical outcroppings of trees on either side. The group had come out of the forest in the lower clearing, which was dominated by water.

The lake, which was deep with a sharp drop off near the shore, was small enough that it was possible to see all edges of it from where they stood. Despite its modest proportions, it was a beautiful lake. The vegetation around it was maintained by human hand, which kept it neat and orderly, but the most eye-catching aspect of it was its colour. Unlike most bodies of water, which were blue-green or brown in the worst cases, the water of the lake here was tinged purple. It gave it an otherworldly effect, watching the violet waves lap gently at the white sand on the shore.

Sioned and Clara marvelled at the sight before them; meanwhile, Eleri grappled with the Water Leaper, trying to gently convince it to let go of her scabbard and return to the water, all without losing a finger to its sharp little teeth.

"Mmm, feel that?" Eleri asked as she managed to bop the Water Leaper on its snout with a single finger, though this only made it squeak at her instead of letting go. "There's still magic here, at least."

At Eleri's words, Clara and Sioned became aware of a curious sensation. It was like a thrumming beneath their skin, a current running through their veins. It wasn't uncomfortable, but rather like the ticking of a clock. Now that they were aware of it, it was all they could think about. Clara even shook her hands out, as if to get rid of the feeling like one does for a pins-and-needles sensation.

"This is magic?" Sioned asked, awed.

"As it should be, as it was all those years ago," Eleri answered, still half-distracted by the creature. "The air here is heavy with ambient magic; it's as present as here as it used to be all over the country before the Great Corruption."

By now, Eleri was walking towards the lake, jiggling her scabbard minutely. This had no effect on the Water Leaper. Clara jogged to keep up with her and Sioned followed at a slower place, head turning to take in everything possible.

"What makes this place so special?" she asked.

"The Keep, over there," Eleri said, jerking a thumb to her right, still looking at the lake.

Sioned turned, and there indeed were the towering, spindly spires and towers of Gryphon's Keep. Focused as she was on the strange lake and its surroundings, Sioned hadn't noticed much beyond the waterfront. Now she turned fully to face the other half of the clearing and was surprised she missed the massive building dominating the sky.

Gryphon's Keep was taller and skinnier than most fortified towers built in castles and sat in the middle of its curtain walls. There were a few other buildings, mostly thin, angular affairs like the keep, though not as tall, clustered around it. It was built out of a strange, purple-black stone, and its jagged appearance seemed menacing, even on that clear, hot autumn day.

"We made it," Sioned breathed out, voice full of awe.

Clara, who had been frowning at Eleri the entire time, never even looked at the Keep. Instead, she stood with her back towards it, clearly ruminating on something.

"Eleri, how can you feel the magic here?" Clara asked, though it was clear from her tone she already knew her answer. "Non-mages can't feel magic."

"Don't start with that again," Eleri said lightly, with an undercurrent of steel to her voice. "I expect that I can feel it because we're so close to the epicentre of modern magic."

"But you've felt ambient magic in other places!" Clara raised her voice, frustrated.

"Other pilgrimage sites! There's bound to be more magic there, too!" Eleri insisted.

Clara gave an annoyed huff and turned to examine the Keep with Sioned, who had tactfully stayed out of their little disagreement. Sioned leaned in so her head was closer to Clara's.

"Best not argue with someone standing ankle-deep in water, losing a fight to a thing like that," she told Clara conspiratorially.

Clara cracked a smile, then seemed to remember she was upset with Sioned as well and fought it down. There was a great splash behind them.

"I am not *losing,*" said Eleri, indignantly.

They both turned to see what Eleri was doing. She was still standing in the shallows, with a damp patch spattered up her left trouser leg—presumably the result of the splash they'd heard. Eleri had the open end of the scabbard tucked under one arm and was using the other to reach for the Water Leaper. She was bent in the middle, her hip-length hair loose and falling into the water around her. Apparently, she was trying to scare the Water Leaper into letting go by drumming her fingers along the scabbard and holding it close to its own habitat for an easy escape.

The Water Leaper glared as balefully as it could, squeaking the entire time. It made no effort to return to the water, or even move at all. If it was a battle of wills, Eleri was, indeed, losing.

"Just leave it alone, Eleri," Sioned advised.

This got Eleri to stand up so quickly, her hair whipped around wildly, sending droplets of water all over all three of them. Her expression was one of disgusted disbelief, and her voice carried the same emotion in it.

"Leave it? It's on my sword! I can't just toss that in the water, it would rust!"

"You could put it on the ground," Clara pointed out sensibly.

Eleri wasn't listening. Her focus was back on the Water Leaper, though she was muttering to herself under her breath, something about her father, lakes, rust, and the sword Excalibur.

Clara rolled her eyes and went to explore around the edge of the lake. Sioned trailed after her, at an awkward distance. It was clear she knew her company wouldn't be welcomed by Clara but she was unwilling to be alone. They walked a quarter of the way around the lake, admiring the plants. The pickleweed was still in bloom, its flowers matching the overall purple colour scheme of the area. There were also bright red cardinals, clumps of sedges and rushes, and arrowhead plants dotted around the water's edge. Clara noted several other kinds of plants, but without flowers she was unable to identify them. Sioned made a few attempts to bring Clara into a conversation about the flowers, but after being thoroughly ignored, she gave up.

When Clara turned to go back, unwilling to go too far from their guide in a new and unusual place, she caught the final stand off between Eleri and the Water Leaper. It all happened too fast for either Clara or Sioned to know what they were seeing in the moment, but the sequence of events was later relayed to them by Eleri.

Eleri, still trying to get the Water Leaper off the end of her scabbard without damage to any involved, had waded further into the lake, up to her knees. She knew the drop-offs in this lake were sharp and unpredictable, so she had shuffled her way forward, feeling out the next step before putting her weight on it. At this moment, she was standing right at the edge of one such drop-off. With her sword still tucked under her left arm, she reached around with her right to dig in her pack. At last, she found a bit of dried meat, and after freeing it from its wrappings, she offered it to the Water Leaper to entice it to drop the scabbard in favour of something edible.

Although not hungry enough to try to eat a human, the Water Leaper couldn't pass up a free treat—but it was unwilling to let go of its other prey. The Water Leaper is a tenacious creature and was perfectly willing to hold fast to Eleri until he was ready to eat her as well. As a creature accustomed to moving by flying, it was unbothered by the way Eleri had been carrying it, but the repeated tapping near its face annoyed it. Now, with Eleri showing it the meat and then moving it away in an attempt to get the Water Leaper to follow it, the creature grew truly irritated.

Just as Eleri realised this, she pulled her hand away again—an instinctive move to get her hands far away from an angry creature with razor-sharp teeth. This was the last straw for the Water Leaper and, gnashing its teeth around the scabbard, it lashed out at Eleri with its tail.

The tail of the Water Leaper is the primary reason it can take down prey so much bigger than its size. This particular one had avoided using it so far, as it wasn't ready to eat Eleri. Now, the long, slender appendage whipped at Eleri, its stinger digging into her shoulder and leaving a deep scratch where it passed through.

Eleri didn't cry out. Instead, she only allowed a sharp intake of breath to express her pain. Then she and the Water Leaper tipped forward and, with a mighty splash, disappeared under the purple water. Clara and Sioned watched, but the only thing to surface was a handful of bubbles.

Just as the two of them were beginning to worry, Sioned had started running back to where Eleri had been. As they rounded the corner, Eleri's head broke the surface. She stood up quickly, sending her hair flying wildly, with water falling off it in streams.

They had barely a moment to see Eleri's face, twisted in a grim mask of determination, before she dived back into the water. Clara and Sioned slowed to a walk but kept their eyes on the spot where Eleri had disappeared again, watching warily. Once again, she stayed beneath the waves longer than they expected her to. When she did come back, Eleri held her sword scabbard over her head in a triumphant pose and a pleased smirk playing about her lips. There were bite marks on the end of it, but the Water Leaper was nowhere to be seen.

As Eleri walked out of the lake, looking quite pleased with herself, it became apparent the Water Leaper had done some real damage with its stinger. Her left arm, still bleeding, hung limp down by her side. As she strode towards Clara and Sioned, it swayed slightly with the movements of her body, but otherwise seemed to be completely disconnected from the rest of Eleri.

Sioned opened her mouth to say something, but the sudden dark look on Eleri's face stopped her. At first, Sioned thought it was due to the uncomfortable revelation of her parentage from earlier, but then a group of people rushed past her and Clara, knocking shoulders with them carelessly. These people, some clad in the robes of the Elders and others in other purple clothes, crowded around Eleri, all speaking at once.

Eleri shrugged them off, as best she could with only one functioning shoulder. Her frown deepened, and she tried many times to be heard over the din, but any words were swiftly drowned out. Her mounting frustration was evident, both on her face and by her body language.

"ENOUGH!" Eleri cried.

Suddenly there was silence. The group clustered around her stopped talking, looking to be a mix of shocked and offended. With her good shoulder, Eleri pushed her way out of the circle to stand beside Sioned and Clara.

"My friends and I have come here for a reason," she started to say, paused to shush whoever tried to interrupt her, and continued. "So why don't we take this inside, and they can get the tour while I visit the physician?"

Despite some grumbling, this was apparently an acceptable proposition, as the people from the Keep started to shuffle back towards the castle. There was a clear attempt to fold Eleri back into the middle of the pack, or at least engage her in conversation, but Eleri stayed resolutely in the middle of Sioned and Clara, singing a cheerful tune loud enough to drown them out. Even Sioned, who was desperately trying to get Eleri to acknowledge her limp and bleeding arm, couldn't get through to her.

And then they were standing at the great gate, built into the curtain wall. Gryphon's Keep towered above the troop of people, cutting a lean, jagged line into the sky. Eleri skipped ahead and spun on her toes to face Sioned and Clara. She gave an exaggerated bow, then stood and gestured above her head with her good arm at the tower.

"Welcome, friends, to Gryphon's Keep."

Chapter Eighteen

Immediately after they walked under the portcullis and through the adjoining door, Eleri was bundled off by the Elders, leaving Clara and Sioned to the junior residents of the Keep. They all stood there, listening to the fading echoes of Eleri's protestations, until the gatehouse was silent again. After that, their new guides, with forced, sickly smiles on their faces, offered Clara and Sioned the tour Eleri had mentioned.

They ushered the women through the bailey, half-heartedly pointing out some of the buildings like the forge, the stables, the bakehouse, and the mews. One young fellow took great delight in sneeringly pointing out the oubliettes to Sioned and Clara. The keep itself—a strange, spindly design uncommon for such a building, but large and fortified nonetheless—sat on a motte, partially obscured by wing walls. They were led through the walls, up the steep incline, and brought into the Great Hall of Gryphon's Keep.

The tour of the interior was again perfunctory, and Sioned and Clara were quickly shuttled along from room to room with little explanation. It was unlikely they would be able to find their way around by themselves—something Eleri would later confirm was intentional.

They were quite glad to see her again, when they were finally brought to the physician's quarters. It was a room with two sections. The first held an array of herbs and tinctures, smelt powerfully, and was cluttered with a desk, a worktable, a small cot, and enough shelves to rival a library. The second, though Sioned and Clara could not see it, was a small infirmary, with six beds available for patients.

Eleri was occupying the small cot in the first room, though she adamantly refused to lay down. She was sitting on the edge, swinging her feet, when Sioned and Clara entered, and waved cheerily at them. The physician, a wizened old man, was hovering around her, trying to encourage or force her to lay down. Eleri took no notice of him.

"Hullo again!" Eleri called out to them. "Back from your tour? They're terrible hosts, aren't they? I'll give you a better one as soon as I escape from here."

The physician gave Eleri a scathing look, but she had already hopped off the cot and made her way over to Sioned and Clara. Her left arm was supported by a sling, and her hand hung lifelessly out of the fabric.

"Goddesses above! What happened to you?" Sioned exclaimed, catching Eleri by the shoulders.

"Don't grab her there!" The old physician snapped.

Sioned jerked her hands back, looking nervous. Eleri gave the physician a dirty look.

"Don't worry about him," she said, looking directly into the physician's eyes. "You didn't grab the cut, and I can't feel it anyway. I can, however, speak for myself."

There was a moment of tense silence, where Clara looked between the physician and Eleri, but then the little brunette turned back to her friends with a grin.

"The Water Leaper's tail has a stinger on it, which releases a paralytic venom so they can trap prey bigger than they are. Luckily, it just barely caught me, so it didn't enter my bloodstream. Just my arm is numb for now, but it should wear off."

Eleri used her right hand to lift her left arm by the sling and drop it during her explanation, showing its complete lack of responsiveness. Then she ushered the two of them out of the physician's chambers with her one hand. As soon as the door closed, Eleri spun to face it, and stuck her tongue out at it. When she caught Clara's disapproving look, she chuckled lightly.

"Childish, I know. But we really don't get along." Then Eleri paused, looking thoughtful. "Though, I suppose I respect old man Gilly in there more than any of the others."

The three of them were walking down the hallway, their steps echoing slightly against the old stone. Clara and Sioned, despite having just been escorted through here, were uncertain, but Eleri strode through the old keep as if she owned it.

"They seemed very concerned about you," hedged Sioned.

Eleri made a strange sound, some mix of a scoff and a laugh.

"My maternal grandfather donates money to the upkeep of the Elders. Significant amounts of money. The underlying agreement is that they, in return, keep an eye on me and try to influence me back to my family."

"That's... nice?" Sioned tried, making Clara snort.

"It's really not," Eleri replied simply.

"It's complicated," Clara guessed.

Eleri made a sour face and made a 'so-so' gesture with her good hand. By this time, she had led them through the twisting halls and stopped in front of a humble wooden door. From her pack, Eleri fished out a small iron key and used it to unlock the door. She opened it with a dramatic flourish.

The room inside was tiny. There was just enough space for a little bed, a squat dresser, and a plain wooden chair tucked in the corner. The dresser was covered in papers, books, and an inkwell in an organisational system unknown to Clara or Sioned. There were little overlapping water rings on the floor beside both the bed and the dresser, from where someone had been in the habit of putting their cups down. The bed, aside from being rather small, was made up with an old, patched quilt in various blues. There was another blanket folded at the end of the bed, and propped up on the pillow tucked under the quilt, there was an old stuffed bear with mismatched button eyes. There was a swath of some kind of periwinkle fabric hung over the back of the chair, half-embroidered with daisies. The needle and thread were still attached, with the needle tucked into the fabric to prevent it from being lost. It was a clean, neat room, but it was stuffed to the brim with things.

Sioned and Clara knew this room belonged to Eleri the moment they crossed the threshold. While the furnishings and other things seemed to fit her well, they were not the main deciding factor. Rather, the amateur mural painted on the ceiling and down the far wall was what made them certain. Painted in patchy shades of midnight blue, it was a reasonably accurate map of the night sky in spring. In the back right corner, above where she'd lay her head at night, was the North Star, Ursa Minor, and Ursa Major. The other stars and constellations radiated out from that point, as if where Eleri slept was the convergence point for the whole scene. As it got further from Eleri's bed, the painting became more precise and steadier. That, along with the array with slightly different shades, led the visitors to the conclusion that Eleri had painted it over time, and the increase in skill came as she grew older. It was the correct assumption.

The three women shuffled in, which was a tight squeeze, until Eleri bade them to sit on the bed while she sat on the rickety old chair. She seemed quite pleased with herself as she watched Clara and Sioned look about her room. Eleri had her good arm thrown over the back of the chair and sat with her legs crossed.

"Welcome to my little corner of Gryphon's Keep," Eleri said, gesturing at the room around them.

"Wow..." Sioned breathed. "You have your own room?"

She was amazed, but Clara merely looked confused.

"Aren't the people who live here generally... mages?" Clara asked. "You've spent your whole life believing you had no magic, so how did this come about?"

"As I said, my family has been involved with the Keep for a very long time. Part of the deal is trying to get me to stay in one place and behave."

Clara snorted, and Eleri flashed her a glittering smile.

"So! If the two of you are still set on what you came here to do, I can help you find the Elders most suited to what you need. The best of the worst, if you will."

"You really don't like the Elders, do you?" Sioned asked.

"Personally? No," Eleri said. "Professionally? No. Aside from their part in my family drama, I believe that being self-proclaimed 'keepers of all magical knowledge' and then hiding themselves away from the people they claim to serve is despicable. That's why I lead as many pilgrims looking for the Keep here as possible—my grandfather's money and influence prevents them from turning me away, and more people get to know about an integral part of themselves and society."

Eleri was quiet for a moment. The far wall had only a small slit of a window, more of an arrow hole than anything else, which she stared out of, deep in thought. When she did finally speak, her voice was far away.

"There was a librarian at the estate my childhood home was a part of—we lived as part of a coven of witches, you see. If it wasn't for that librarian and her willingness to share what she knew, I would have never realised I was in danger, or that the way my mother treated me wasn't my fault. Which is why it makes my blood boil when these so-called Elders hoard all the research about magic they can and refuse to allow other mages into their circle."

There was little either visitor had to say after a pronouncement like that. Eleri had them store their possessions in the meagre space under her bed and lead them on a much more in-depth tour of the keep. This tour ended at the library—a cavernous room set in the middle of the tower with multiple levels. There were no actual windows, as the keep had been originally built to withstand sieges, but there were large faux-windows, each magically displaying a different scene. They could be changed to show whatever location one wanted, though only an exterior view.

Sioned, in a fit of homesickness, went up to one after Eleri's explanation and put her hand gently to where the pane would be.

It gave a gel-like ripple, and the image shifted to show a large manor house, sitting in between a vineyard and a curated garden. She stood there and watched as a young boy, who looked very similar to Sioned, exited the house and began playing some sort of imaginative game with himself. Sioned watched, her eyes growing glassy but smiling all the while, until Clara gently led her away.

The bottom level of the library, where they were standing, had some large tables interspersed within the bookshelves. Eleri had, in her usual fashion, commandeered one. When Clara and Sioned joined her, Sioned discreetly wiping at her eyes, Eleri already had a piece of paper and a quill at the ready.

"We'll need a plan. Let's make sure we know exactly what we're looking for to narrow down the search."

Eleri pointed the back end of the quill at Clara.

"Clara. You want to wholly give up your magic, correct?" At Clara's nod, Eleri jotted it down in her notes, then continued. "That won't be difficult. It's not talked about much these days, but the Elders *have* found a way to do that and do it with frequency."

Clara jolted in her seat.

"They do? I came here because I heard a rumour there might be a way, and hoped the Elders might help me find it."

Eleri crinkled her nose. She doodled a little star on the corner of the paper, then looked up at Clara. Her mouth was twisted in an expression of distaste.

"Yes. They know. Most people don't like to talk about it, since magic is so rare now, and needed more than ever. But the Elders believe it's better to give the magic back to the world rather than 'waste' it on people who don't appreciate it."

Clara was quiet. Her face was downturned, making it difficult to see her expression. From what was visible, one could see her bottom lip trembling.

"I just want.... To be what my family expects..." Clara's voice was thick with shame.

Both Eleri and Sioned took one of Clara's hands in their own. Sioned held it tenderly, like Clara was the most precious thing in the world. Eleri held it tight, as if she could lend her strength to Clara through the force of her grip.

"Waste, they say, as if they haven't made magic a burden now," Eleri said derisively. "Not everyone is willing or able to devote themselves to their magic like they're forced to now. Never mind all that, Clara. You have every right to decide what you want for yourself."

Clara gave a little laugh, though it was wet with unshed tears.

"You have very strong opinions about all this, don't you?"

"About what matters, yes," Eleri responded lightly.

There was a moment of silence. Sioned continued holding Clara's hand, as the other woman either didn't notice or care to take it back, despite the current rocky state of their relationship. Eleri scribbled a few more sentences down, then abruptly turned to Sioned.

"And you, you said you want to join the Keep as a researcher?"

Sioned hesitated, then said with conviction, "I do. I really liked what you said about the different expressions of magic between casters; I'd like to investigate that more."

Eleri nodded absently, writing that down. At the sound of the heavy main doors opening, her head whipped around, and Eleri's face lit up. Sioned and Clara turned to see what had brought the smile to her face, and it was a middle-aged woman, her red hair streaked with soft grey, who had just entered the library. She was dressed in the deep purple robes of the Elders.

"This is exactly who we want to see!" Eleri told her companions.

She then half-raised herself out of her seat and raised an arm to beckon the woman over.

"Hullo, Catrin! Won't you please come over and meet my friends? We could use your help with something."

Chapter Nineteen

The next week frequently saw Eleri alone in the library. It was not an unusual situation for her, and she passed it intently researching the great loss of magic. Her strange experience in the oak tree clearing had yet to leave her mind, despite being dismissed by every Elder she spoke to about it. The extensive library Gryphon's Keep kept her fully immersed in her topic, and there was plenty of practical and theoretical works for Eleri to work her way through.

There were only two things that were able to pull her away. One was when Sioned or Clara came to visit her, however perfunctory on their part it felt. Now that Eleri had introduced them to the necessary people, they were both undergoing serious discussions about their chosen paths. They had largely devoted themselves to their task, now that both of their dreams were within reach, which made casual conversation rare. After such close proximity with them left during their trip, this disconnect left Eleri feeling bereft, which had never happened with anyone else she'd played guide to, strangely enough.

The second thing that Eleri pulled herself away from her research for was practice. Clara's words had rattled around in her head ever since the forest, and Eleri was cautiously optimistic about trying magic again. When not in the library, she spent many hours tucked away in her room, trying out different conduits. As before, there was no reaction no matter what she tried.

When it grew too upsetting to bear, or the pain from her still healing arm was too distracting, Eleri would escape to the bailey to wander in the fresh air. Winter was almost upon the Keep, the air growing crisp and cool, finally. It was a welcome change to Eleri, who had long grown tired of the sweltering autumn weather.

One overcast day found Eleri lying on her back, hidden behind the old armoury. Unused as it was, the building gave Eleri perfect cover from prying, disapproving eyes. She had brought a few books out with her and had been taking notes all that morning, but for the moment she was simply looking at shapes in the clouds. Thinking distantly of the stars, Eleri raised her hand and snapped her fingers, wishing she could see them and pretending the snap would make it possible.

It did. Little lights, glittering like distant stars, winked into existence and floated above her head. Eleri sat straight up. The lights did not disappear, not even when she touched one gently with the tip of her finger. Eleri held one of the lights gently in the palm of her hand, enthralled. There had been no need for a conduit or any spell—which Eleri would later attribute to being born of a father from before the Great Corruption, whose bloodline was not yet drained of magic—it had simply been Eleri and the faith someone else had in her. The Trials, the Elders, her mother, everyone had been wrong about her. Eleri let the conjured stars float about, practicing summoning and dismissing them until she was exhausted.

There in the bailey, watching birds soar through the air, is where Sioned found her that day. Her long brown hair was fluttering in the wind, as was the blue ribbons twined in it. Sioned was tucked into a cloak against the late autumn air, but Eleri stood there in just the long sleeves of her tunic. The two women stood in silence, tracking the movements of the bird with their eyes.

"Why do you stay?" Sioned finally asked, breaking the silence but not the tension.

"Clara will need a guide to find her way home," Eleri replied. "Besides, I'm still not ready to give up on my research into the vanishing magic. I know the Elders say it's in my head, or the result of weak mages overexerting themselves, but that doesn't satisfy me. I think there's something more they're not saying."

"I think you're too distrustful, especially of authority. You say they hoard knowledge, but they've done nothing but answer my questions about their way of life since I got here. Maybe you expect too much."

Sioned left her there, walking stiffly back into the Keep.

Eleri had supper alone that evening, her mood low after the talk with Sioned earlier. There was always a large meal served communally in the Great Hall, which people would drift in and out of. Eleri had been eating there, isolated despite hoping to see her friends, but this night she served herself a plate right at the end of mealtime and took it out to the ramparts. Tucked up against the parapets, Eleri reflected on how quickly her friendship with Clara and Sioned had soured. It even dampened the thrill of finally being able to magic, as she had always dreamed of.

Despite their haphazard beginning, Eleri had warmed to Clara and Sioned faster than she usually did to new people, maybe because she saw some of her own struggles in them. It made it all the more heartbreaking for them to turn on her as suddenly as they did. The Elders of Gryphon Keep had done their best to envelop Sioned and Clara into their folds, leaving Eleri on the outside looking in, as always. It felt deliberate, and Eleri felt small in a way she hadn't since leaving her mother's house.

Eleri took the plate down to the kitchens, sneaking in through an old servants' door to avoid detection. It was late enough that anyone with the kitchen shift would berate her for bringing more dishes when they were supposed to be finished cleaning. It wasn't a fair move, Eleri knew, but she wasn't up to dealing with anyone else, too lost in her own head. Luckily, the kitchen was dark and empty, so Eleri quickly washed her plate and utensils and left them to dry. After leaving, she wandered aimlessly through the lower castle. Lost in thought as she was, it was almost inevitable that she would trip, and so she did.

Knelt on the floor, Eleri rubbed at her knee where she had banged it against the unforgiving stone. So close to the ground, she was able to feel the slight breeze coming from where the wall and the floor met. With a frown of confusion, Eleri felt along the seam, surprised by the strength and chill of the air current. If her mental map was accurate, there wouldn't be anything on the other side of the wall, aside from the cliff face this portion of the Keep was built into.

Just as Eleri was about to stand, there was a strange clicking sound, and a bright light in the shape of a rectangle etched itself into the stonework. The part of the wall she was pressing on sank inwards for a moment, then suddenly swung out into the hall, making Eleri throw herself to the side to avoid being hit. There was a rush of cold, stale air, and Eleri found herself on the floor, staring into the entrance of a tunnel she'd never seen before.

In many instances, a sudden cave is a cause for retreat. For help, new equipment, to inform others of a new danger, or at least let someone know where you're going in case you don't make it back. In this case, Eleri had no one she felt comfortable relying on in that way and had a sneaking suspicion that any mention of this tunnel would result in it being heavily covered up, and none of her questions answered.

Slowly, Eleri got to her feet, looking up and down the hall to ensure there was no one else around. When she was sure she was alone—and she was, so late at night in a barely-used corridor—Eleri slipped through the heavy stone door. After a few moments of fishing around in the dark, she found a large enough stone to act as a door stopper, propped the door open just the barest amount, and started forward. She was giddy at the prospect of finding and exploring an unknown area of Gryphon's Keep—perhaps this was a siege tunnel, unused and forgotten since the Keep's days as a true castle and stronghold.

Out of habit, Eleri felt her way through the dark, hand along the wall and gently toeing the floor before committing to a full step. With a soft chuckle—one part at herself, and the other at how strange her life felt now—Eleri raised a hand and called forth her little light. Like before, it was a small, white-blue thing, somewhat diamond-shaped, like a simple drawing of a star or sparkle. Even when Eleri lowered her hand, it floated gently around her head, illuminating the path ahead. Two more identical lights joined the first, all circling lazily around Eleri like a personal constellation.

The moment the cool light flooded the tunnel, Eleri noticed something that made her stomach drop to her feet. The floor of the tunnel was worn down in the middle, a clear path made by feet passing though often, and probably in great numbers. It was, perhaps, not an old and disused siege tunnel after all.

Eleri tried to rationalise it to herself. Maybe, in the times before the history she knew, the tunnels beneath the Keep were frequently used—daily, even!—and that was the reason for the wear etched into the stone. Even as she thought about all the different ways the tunnels could have been used, the conclusion that the Elders were using this tunnel for some secret purpose had already made its home in her mind.

It wasn't even that the Elders were keeping their activities from *her*, specifically. There was no love lost between them, and for the majority of her life she had been an outsider parasite to their circle. Even if she believed magic knowledge deserved to be shared, the current policy of the Keep was to keep it for mages only. But that it had been hidden behind a secret door in a frequently empty hall seemed... Unusual, if not truly suspicious.

The chill in the air grew steadily as Eleri made her way through the tunnels. There was a definitive slope to them, taking her deeper and deeper into the cliff side. There was a faint pounding, though Eleri wasn't sure if it was real or just the blood rushing in her ears. She wished she had thought to grab a cloak or something, but she had been so caught up in her discovery that the chill of the cave hadn't even crossed her mind. The path was getting steeper, and the fact that it was worn smooth made it slippery—Eleri's foot slid almost out from underneath her more than once.

The thudding grew louder. It was rhythmic, almost hypnotic, similar to the one-two beat of her heart, even if now Eleri realised it was an external sound. As she approached an opening at the end of the tunnel, the sound was almost deafening, and the ground pulsed in time with each beat. Eleri rounded the corner, entering a cavern filled with white crystals that glowed faintly, which were the only source of illumination present. The floor of the cavern, which was not natural, and was paved with large flat stones, was not as worn down as the tunnel itself had been. It was still worn and evidently trodden-on frequently, but it was more dispersed and obviously maintained.

Eleri peered around the cavern cautiously. To her left was the end of the chamber and to her right was a long stone dais, which separated the cavern roughly in half. There was a small offshoot on the other side of the cavern, where the thudding sound originated from, but Eleri couldn't see into it. There was a purple curtain that hid it from view. The cavern was devoid of people.

Still wary, not just of the strange cave itself but also whatever was the source of the rhythmic pounding, Eleri crept slowly around the room. There was little on the floor or the walls of the chamber, only the benign marks of frequent use Eleri had already noted. Closer to the dais, there were platforms along the wall. They were clearly artificial, as they were completely symmetrical and overlooked the dais perfectly.

It was the dais that gave Eleri pause. There were dark stains that were splattered along the length of the surface and dripped down the sides. Some of the stains were set into the stone, and some had some brownish flakes peeling off. Eleri reached out as if to touch the stains, but something inside her kept her from doing so. Her hand, outstretched above the dais, hovered in the air for a moment and then pulled back.

Even without touching the stone itself, Eleri was able to examine it. Although partially obscured by the stains and some wear, she could make out some runes carved into the stone. She gestured, bringing the little lights closer to the dais, and squinted in the dim illumination at the markings. Unlike the stains, the majority of the markings were focused around the base of the dais.

Eleri knelt down and put her hand out to steady herself. It had been an unconscious movement, but the second Eleri put her hand to the dais there was a strong shock that traveled up her arm. Instantly, Eleri leapt up and away. Even after the sharp pain faded, a strange lack of feeling in her arm. It was similar to the lingering sensation of numbness in the left shoulder and arm as a result of the Water Leaper's stinger.

She gave her hand a shake, as if she could force feeling back into it that way, and flexed her fingers and elbow. There was no pain with the movement, but it was stiff and difficult to control. Eleri gave the dais a frown; her quick examination of the runes showed that they were unfamiliar to her, but the strange shock suggested that they were not something she wanted to play around with. Her first instinct was to record them in her ever-present notebook, but then a dark thought came to her mind. Eleri wondered if the runes, which were so painful to the touch, would make her notebook unusable. Besides, such repulsive magic was probably not one she was keen to repeat—especially not knowing the effects. Instead, Eleri drifted towards the curtain behind the dais. She was partly lost in thought about what she had already found, and partly distracted by the loud thudding sound. It was so powerful that the floor beneath her feet was shaking in time with it. As Eleri approached the curtain, the same sense of repulsiveness that made her wary to touch the dais was there but magnified a thousand times. Even just looking at the purple fabric made her sick to her stomach.

Eleri steeled herself and tore the curtain away. As soon as she did, the sense of nothingness settled around her. It was the same deadening of the air that she had experienced in little bursts when magic failed, and in totality when at the great oak tree pilgrimage site. For whatever reason, there was a complete lack of magic here, and had been for some time.

When she had opened the curtain, Eleri had instinctively closed her eyes. Maybe it was in response to the loss of her senses, or fear, or maybe it was because of the overwhelming noise. Now, she opened them again, and her blood ran cold.

As Eleri stood there, one hand still grasping the curtain for support, she stared up at the giant heart that overfilled the little chamber. It was easily taller than three men stacked one on top of the other and was the source of the noise. It beat like a regular heart, and something flowed within it, though only some of the arteries and veins burrowed into the stone around it. The rest ended suddenly, like they had been cut, but nothing spilled from them. The actual heart was blood red, with sickly dark lines scattered across the surface, like an infection had taken hold. The heart gave a heaving shudder, then continued its normal beat. Eleri felt as if she was being drawn in, and almost crossed the threshold, but some deep instinct told her to run, and so she did, all the way back up the tunnel to the corridor, her heart beating in time with the one in the cave the entire way.

Chapter Twenty

Eleri ran full tilt until she was in her room. Uncaring if anyone saw her, she slammed the door shut, and dropped to the floor, her back pressed against the wood, as if that would ward off the terrible experience she just had. Her lungs felt tight, and she was wheezing slightly. Eleri put her head between her knees, hoping to quell the nausea brought on by her breathlessness. It didn't help and made Eleri feel as if she were choking, so she uncurled a little to rest her head back against the door.

For a long while, Eleri focused only on getting her breathing back under control. Even when it was, she stayed where she was sitting, eyes closed, trying to decide her next move. The shock and fear coursing through her veins left her wired but exhausted, which was exacerbated by the lung attack she'd just had. Staggering like she was half-dead, Eleri rose and crossed to her little bed, dropping face-first onto the mattress. She didn't bother to undress or even crawl under the covers, and despite the jittery feelings still left over, fell asleep almost instantly.

The sun was just rising in the sky when consciousness abruptly found Eleri. There was no gentle waking today, just the change from sleep to wakefulness from one breath to another. Her eyes snapped open, and Eleri pushed herself into a standing position before her body even knew it was fully awake. She stood still for a second, letting her body catch up with her mind, then was back into action again.

After quickly washing and changing her clothes, Eleri strapped her sword to her waist and all but charged through the halls. Multiple people called after her, reminding her of the 'no weapons' policy of the Keep, but she never acknowledged them. One or two people tried to grab her arm, to stop her or remove the sword themselves, but Eleri slipped through their fingers with ease.

She threw the doors to the great hall open. There were only a few people inside, mostly those on serving duty that morning who were setting the tables, but a few others were already waiting for breakfast as well. Most jumped when the heavy doors flew open, and a few turned to frown at Eleri for disturbing the early morning peace.

These frowns turned to true expressions of disappointment or disgust when they saw the sword at her hip, but Eleri paid them no mind. She strode through the tables and took the platform at the head of the room, where the throne and high table had once sat. Once breakfast started, it would be used as a buffet table, but now Eleri guarded it, commandeering attention with her position and domineering body language. The hall went immediately silent, as if they had, as a group, decided to hold their breath. A few Elders and other scholars made to stand up, but Eleri glared them back into their seats.

"There's something evil under the Keep."

Despite her small stature, Eleri cut an imposing figure at the head of the hall. Her arms were on her hips and her face was set in a neutral, regal mask. She surveyed the few people in front of her, and was dismayed to see that there was little, if any, surprise on their faces.

"I see from your expressions that you already know this," Eleri said, voice filled with seething disappointment. "Pity that you never seem to share your information."

There was now some murmuring among the crowd, partly due to their reaction and partly due to the newcomers filing in and getting filled in. No one had a chance to say anything further, however, before the Head Elder, Alphius, came hurrying into the great hall, some of his advisors trailing behind him.

It was not unexpected. Eleri had seen more than one person send a magical missive to their leader when she took her metaphorical podium. She stood tall, keeping a watchful, cold eye on the scurrying Elders.

The old man, with his grey hair and his once tailored robes came to a stop before Eleri. Although he was a tall, spindly man, they were nearly eye-level with one another. She had positioned herself above him, on the platform that once held royalty. Even being two steps above gave her an edge on him.

His face was as dour as it ever was. His hair, once jet black, was shot through with streaks of grey. There had been a twinkle in his eye when Eleri had been young, but as she grew and idolised him less, any sparkle he had once was now dimmed. He was no longer the kindly old man of her youth; now he was just old.

"I found the tunnel, in the corridor off the kitchens," Eleri told Alphius. Her voice was clear and strong, and it rang out across the hall.

There was a collective intake of breath from the assorted Elders in the room, but Alphius himself made no response. He watched her for a moment, studying Eleri, then put on a warm but artificial smile.

"Come down from there, young lady. Let's talk about this privately."

Eleri did not dignify this with a response beyond a toss of her head and setting her gaze resolutely over Alphius' shoulder.

When it became apparent Eleri had no desire to answer him, Alphius sighed rather theatrically. He raised a placating hand and beckoned her forward.

"Eleri, let's go. There's no need to concern yourself with this; it's a magical matter." The tone Alphius used may have once passed for that of a grandfatherly mentor, but there was an underlying hardness that belayed his annoyance.

Eleri's reserved expression did not change. Without missing a beat, she flung her arm—the right, as the left was still a bit slow to respond—out and snapped her fingers. The flames of every candle in the room roared upwards, glowing a brilliant blue. No one spoke until the flames calmed back to their natural state.

A lone voice piped up from the ever-growing crowd, sounding both aghast and amazed.

"How did she *do* that?"

Eleri rolled her eyes. She cocked her hip out to the side and put her hands on her hips.

"As it turns out, I've always had magic. Your Trials were simply unequipped to demonstrate it." Eleri paused and scanned the hall with her eyes. She could see that there were many disbelieving faces, and some looking confused or upset. Clara, though, stood out to her, as the blonde had a rather smug expression on her face. "I suppose it would be fair to say that the Elders are *not* as all-knowing about magic as they would like to appear."

Alphius closed his eyes, looking old beyond even his advanced years. When he opened them again, there was a light behind them, not quite cruel or malicious, but not friendly either. He stepped up onto the platform, uncomfortably close to Eleri, but she refused to give him the satisfaction of stepping away.

She jutted her chin out, looking stubbornly up into Alphius' face. He placed a cold, leathery hand on each of her shoulders. It sent a shiver up her spine, but she did her best not to show it.

"Listen, young Eleri. It may be hard for you to conceive of, but there is more at play here than you could possibly imagine. You ought not to be so entitled, to want to be a part of everything. The Elders know of what you speak and are already working towards a solution. Enjoy your magic; I know you've dreamed of this for a long time."

With that, Alphius gave Eleri a gentle push, encouraging her off the platform. Cheeks burning red with humiliation, Eleri went and left the great hall altogether.

Eleri was face down on her bed when Clara and Sioned came to find her. Her unmoving body made Clara pause for a second, but Sioned simply shoved Eleri over so that there was enough room for her to sit on the edge of the bed. When Clara made a noise of concern in the back of her throat, Sioned gave the most 'older sister' expression the blonde had ever seen on her face.

"She's not *dead*, she's having a sulk," Sioned explained, exasperated.

"And?" Eleri asked her pillow, her voice coming out muffled by it. "Mind your own business."

Sioned prodded Eleri's hip again. This time, Eleri twisted so that she could look at Sioned. Her blue eyes were ringed in red and there were dried tears on her face as well as red lines from where the pillow had pressed into her skin. She looked rather pathetic, and certainly defeated.

"Come on, then," Sioned said bracingly. "Sit up, clean your face—I know you have a kerchief somewhere—there's a girl."

Eleri had pulled herself up to sit cross-legged. There was a slight pout on her face, and she looked at Sioned with irritation.

"I'm not one of your little sisters. You don't need to come fuss at me," Eleri said, still sniffling slightly.

"Are you sure about that?" Sioned laughed lightly. "You look exactly like the little moppets after a scolding right now."

Sioned reached out and tucked a wayward bit of fringe behind Eleri's ear. It had been stuck to the dried tears, and Eleri grimaced at the sensation when Sioned tugged it free.

"Now, then. What's this all about? Isn't it a bit of an overreaction?" Sioned asked, sensibly.

Clara, still standing awkwardly in the door, winced. Eleri's face first crumpled, then reshaped itself into a blank mask.

"There is a giant, beating heart under Gryphon's Keep. It is siphoning the magic from the air, and it is poised directly in the centre of the magical community. And they tell me to leave it, dismiss me like a child."

"Well..." Clara said uncertainly, "*Aren't* you barely more than a child?"

Sioned shot a glare over her shoulder at Clara. It distinctly said she was being unhelpful.

"When my father just was fifteen..." Eleri trailed off, and visibly deflated, her shoulders hunching and her voice growing smaller. "Alas. I am not my father."

There was a brief silence, then Eleri roared back to life. She sprung up, so that she was standing on her bed.

"And yet! I am not an idiot, but I have been denied by the Elders again and again! Even now, when I could be considered part of their community, they push me away!"

Eleri hopped down from the bed and began pacing in tight circles in the free space of the room. Clara was forced to join Sioned on the bed, unwilling to be in the way of Eleri and her pent-up energy.

Eleri's voice remained at an even tone and volume, but she began speaking quicker and quicker.

"Call me entitled! As if I have no business being concerned about something that could affect our entire way of life. Perhaps I cannot fix it on my own, but do I not have a duty to myself and others to try and better our circumstances? Put me to work on the problem! I want to help!"

Eleri stopped as suddenly as she began. In a small voice, barely audible, she echoed herself.

"I just want to help."

"So help," Clara said simply. When Eleri whipped around to stare at her, Clara shrugged. "You've never needed anyone's permission before; why start now?"

"Even if you don't help solve this problem, isn't doing something better than nothing?" Sioned asked. "Maybe you don't research... whatever that big heart is, maybe you pick a different topic. Or keep bringing people to the Keep, and one of them cracks the mystery. I know your family might not believe you're more than a mistake, and you might too, that doesn't mean you can't at least *try* to help, right?"

As her friends spoke, Eleri's smile grew until it was a full-blown beam. She bounded forward and kissed both Clara and Sioned on their foreheads; it was quick but filled with emotions.

"Thank you. Truly. I needed to hear that," Eleri told them tenderly. She all but raced to the door, and threw it open, barely remembering to call over her shoulder. "I'll be in the library if you need me!"

And with that, she disappeared down the hall, not quite running, but definitely striding with purpose.

Sioned smiled after her until the sounds of her booted feet on the stone floors had long since faded away. She then turned that smile on Clara.

"I suppose that was *us* doing our part to help the world," she said jokingly.

Her smile fell off her face when she remembered that Clara was distant from her now. But Clara turned her head, regarded Sioned with a serious expression, then took Sioned's hand from where it rested on the bed. Clara licked her lips nervously.

"I... have nothing to offer you. Even if I wasn't disowned, my family is small, and not very well-off. I know nothing of being a lady or a merchant, or how to run a business like yours. I know I am in no way your equal, but..."

Clara paused, looking embarrassed. She took a deep breath to steady herself, then looked into Sioned's eyes.

"I think... No. I know I love you. You just proved that you're everything I want. I want to spend every day with you. It would be a privilege to breathe the same air as you. I will spend every day improving myself until I am worthy of holding your hand. I—"

Sioned interrupted, holding up their linked hands, and gave Clara's a tight squeeze. Her eyes were shiny.

"Clara, I don't ever want you to let go."

And there they sat, alone in Eleri's tiny room, staring into each other's eyes in delight, new understanding passing between them.

Chapter Twenty-One

It was clear that Eleri's renewed fervour was unappreciated by the Elders and other residents of Gryphon's Keep. When she wasn't consumed by her research—sitting so still she could have been a statue if not for the turning of the page—she flitted between the library shelves with almost manic energy. If neither of those two pastimes satisfied her, Eleri would be found wandering the bailey, singing under her breath. Some of the songs were recognisable, others seemed to be Eleri's own composition—often about whatever she had been reading that day.

Sioned and Clara could admit they understood where the Elders were coming from, but it was so nice for them to see Eleri lively again that they couldn't bring themselves to object. She'd seemed so defeated during their stay. One thing Clara noted was that Eleri hadn't sung since they arrived at the Keep, until now. The sound of her lilting voice, which had been a constant companion in the forests and little villages, had essentially vanished the second they crossed the threshold of Gryphon's Keep. It had almost seemed like someone else had taken Eleri's place, someone quiet and mousy.

Eleri's discovery of the strange heart beneath the Keep had thrown Clara and Sioned's plans from the window. Elders were now on edge, though whether it was from the unbridled disgust Eleri radiated when she was near them, the ferocious way in which she devoured magical reference books, or something else, it was difficult to tell. Sioned and Clara had been pushed by the wayside—each of their mentors had cited an unforeseen increase in workload, though Clara insisted they were being pushed out due to their proximity to Eleri. Sioned maintained that Clara had been taken in by Eleri's anti-authoritarian position.

Not that either of them were devastated by their new free time. Though they used some of it to check in with Eleri more so than they had been, the majority was for themselves. The bailey and surrounding lands of Gryphon's Keep were well-maintained and manicured, and provided an excellent backdrop for the new lovers to stroll around and converse.

Clara and Sioned were doing just that, walking arm-in-arm past the mews, when a voice from the shadows caught their attention.

"Psst, Clara!" It was Marcus, one of the researchers at the Keep. He had been peripherally involved in helping Clara with her plan to give up her magic. Now he stood half-hidden behind the mews, and his voice almost drowned out by the sounds of the birds. Curious, Clara came closer to him, Sioned trailing slightly behind. When Clara was close enough, Marcus continued in a whisper.

"If you still want to get rid of your magic, we can help you with that tonight. Then you can go back home to your regular life."

Clara brightened, but then her smile dimmed as she looked back at Sioned. Sioned tried to look encouraging.

"If it's what you want, then do it. I want you to be happy." She came up closer to Clara and tucked their arms together again. "And if you want to go, I'd go with you. I'll support you in anything you choose."

"You don't have to do that," Clara protested, but the rest was drowned out by Marcus.

"Not sure if Sioned can come with you, you know. The process is very, uh, delicate and we wouldn't want to upset it."

Something about the way Marcus spoke set Clara on edge, but she agreed to his conditions nonetheless. After he left, Sioned looked a little put out, until Clara told her that she'd make sure Sioned was there, too, even if she had to have Eleri sneak her in.

Luckily, Marcus directed Clara to come find him in two days' time. That gave the pair of them time to try to convince Marcus and the others to allow Sioned to attend. When that didn't work, they brought the issue to Eleri.

Eleri was immediately on board with sneaking Sioned into the ceremony. By her own admission, she had watched many initiation and other ceremonies at the Keep in her life, following the processions through unused servants' corridors and hiding in unseen corners.

It was suspicious, however, to Eleri when Clara told her that the ceremony was to be held late at night. In all her years knowing the Elders, they had held anything important—meetings, initiation rituals, ceremonies—in broad daylight. The Elders were a proud group of people and were unashamed of their actions, wanting every to see their magnificent acts of magic.

Sioned thought Eleri was being paranoid, spurred on by her recent discovery and rejection. Clara offered the idea that the Elders, being so fond of magic, did find it shameful to renounce it—though she said it with a twisted, wry expression.

Neither of these explanations soothed Eleri's nerves, but she did her best to bury her concerns to be able to be there for her friends.

On the appointed night, Clara dressed in the loose, comfortable clothes she was directed to wear. All three were sitting in the little guest room Clara had claimed. The couple orbited around each other, helping each other prepare for the night, while Eleri sat on the bed, lost in thought. Sioned, dressed in the best shirt she'd packed as a sign of support, shared one last kiss with her before Marcus came to lead Clara away.

Eleri and Sioned waited for a moment longer until the sound of the footsteps faded almost completely away, then slipped out of Clara's room after them. At the end of the corridor, there was a small, simple wooden door which led to the servants' hidden hallway. With a practised air, Eleri opened it slowly, keeping the unoiled hinges from squealing too loudly.

Once they were inside the dark corridor, Eleri summoned her little star lights, and she and Sioned set off. They followed Clara and Marcus by the noises they made walking and by Clara helpfully keeping up an animated discussion. The muffled sounds of her and Marcus' voices came through the stone walls, which allowed Eleri and Sioned to ensure they were on the same path. The three of them hadn't discussed that beforehand, it was simply Clara's impromptu way of ensuring Sioned would be there with her. By giving Eleri and Sioned something more audible than footsteps, Clara hoped to keep Sioned from missing even a second of the ceremony. However, it turned out to be more necessary than expected. Rather than going to the Great Hall, the highest tower of the Keep, or any of the other places Eleri expected the ceremony to take place, Marcus led Clara to the basement.

With trepidation, Eleri brought Sioned through the maze-like servant halls that criss-crossed behind the scenes of the basement, until the lack of a continued path made them exit into the dark kitchen. They padded silently between the preparation tables, ovens, and stoves, until they came to the main door of the room.

Eleri pressed her ear to the door, listening to the receding sounds of Marcus and Clara. She brought her one hand up and snapped her fingers—a sound that seemed to reverberate through the empty kitchen. The little star lights drifting around her winked out of existence. She waited a moment longer, then gently eased the door open.

Eleri's head popped out into the darkened corridor from behind the kitchen door like a rabbit poking its head out of its burrow. When she saw no one else—just the fading light of Marcus and Clara's torches disappearing around the bend—Eleri waved Sioned forward with her. They crept cautiously in the dark, taking the utmost care to silence their footsteps and their breathing.

Sioned and Eleri followed along like this, each step making Eleri's heart feel colder. It was the same path Eleri had taken when she found the secret tunnel that Marcus led Clara down now. Her stomach dropped to her feet and Eleri grabbed Sioned's hand and held on tightly when Marcus stopped and opened that very same tunnel entrance.

Though they could only see her back, Sioned and Eleri could see the way that Clara tensed. She still allowed Marcus to usher her along the steep, worn path, but there was the faintest trembling in her hands.

Eleri allowed Marcus and Clara to disappear down the hall. She held Sioned steady until the door was almost completely shut, then darted forward to catch it before it could latch. Sioned and Eleri squeezed through the smallest gap possible, then made their way down the treacherous path, hand-in-hand.

Clara had stopped her aimless chatting, but there was no need for it now—there was only one path to take. Feeling like children wandering the halls after bedtime, looking for a parent in the wake of a nightmare, Eleri and Sioned followed the pair.

The lights in the cavern were nearly blinding, even before they were properly in the room. Eleri and Sioned stopped just before the cavern opened into the room, Eleri shading her eyes with her free hand. The people in the room were facing away towards the dais, which was now laid with a white cloth, but Eleri still directed Sioned to crouch with her in the shadows.

From this obscured position, they saw Marcus deliver Clara to Alphius, who directed her to lay on her back on the dais. Clara did so, looking stiff and uncomfortable. Eleri gripped Sioned's hand so hard it was beginning to hurt, but neither cared. They all but held their breath, kneeling in the dirt and dark as the world around them was shook by the beating of the giant heart.

One of the Elders reached for the curtain that separated the room from the heart, and Eleri shifted minutely. Sioned didn't pay much attention to her, assuming that Eleri was just looking for a more comfortable position. Sioned's eyes were locked on Clara, who had grown pale with fear. She was so tense she had stopped trembling.

Two things then happened simultaneously. An attendant—differentiated from the Elders by the lighter colour of their robe—raised a wicked looking knife above where Clara lay, and Eleri darted forward. The only sensation that gave Sioned a clue that the younger girl was moving was the feeling of her hand slipping from Sioned's grip. Otherwise, she would have sworn that Eleri simply appeared next to the dais.

Still low to the ground, Eleri jabbed the attendant behind the knee. When they crumpled to the ground with a shout, she rolled to the far end of the dais and grabbed Clara by the ankle. Clara sat up in surprise. It was as if time ground to a halt at that moment. Clara sat still, the attendant laid motionless on the ground, and from the corner of her eye, Eleri could see the curtain obscuring the Heaving Heart from view frozen in the air as if something unseen held it aloft.

Eleri didn't give herself time to ponder this before she was pulling the blonde off the stone to the floor next to her. As Clara came off the edge of the dais, Eleri's hand came up to brace her neck and base of her skull. When Clara hit the floor, time seemed to speed back up to its regular tempo again, and suddenly everything was in motion.

Clara had just cleared the surface of the dais when something smashed into the stone. It was one of the veins of the heart, mottled with purple and green and moving sinuously. The force of its impact had cracked the stone of the dais, leaving a depression and spiderweb cracks on the surface.

Clara stared at the damage in horror. If Eleri had not moved her, the vein would have landed directly on her chest—and likely would have smashed her rib cage into pieces. Clara sat there, watching the vein root around on the dais, even as Eleri rose to confront the Elders swarming towards them, and only moved when Sioned came from the shadows to tug her away.

Alphius reached them first. Eleri noted distantly that he, too, gave the searching vein a large berth. He grabbed Eleri by the shoulders with a bruising grip and tugged her close to get in her face.

"You little nightmare!" he snared, sour breath rushing over Eleri's face with every word. "You just have to stick your fingers in everything, don't you?"

"You were going to kill my friend!" Eleri yelled back. "Even if I hadn't been here, do you think there wouldn't be questions tomorrow morning when Clara didn't show up for breakfast?"

The vein, having thoroughly investigated the dais and found nothing, lunged for Clara and Sioned. They managed to tumble out of the way, which made Alphius and Eleri the next closest target. When he noticed this, Alphius shoved Eleri towards it, but she just dropped to the floor and allowed the vein to dart above her head.

Alphius, the Elders, and the attendants stumbled back from the vein as well. Sitting on the floor, with her back to the dais, Eleri watched genuine fear flash across their faces. Doing her best to call no attention to herself, she moved to her hands and knees and slowly crawled towards where Sioned and Clara were pressed against the wall in fear.

As soon as she was close enough, Eleri put a hand on each of their faces and cradled their cheeks gently.

"Have no fear," she told them solemnly. "I brought you here, so I will ensure you get home safely."

Marcus overheard this.

"There is nothing you can do! The Heaving Heart has been awoken, and now it demands a sacrifice!" He shouted, voice shrill with fear.

Eleri threw a dirty look at him over her shoulder, then stood straight and proud beside the dais. The others were, like Sioned and Clara, huddled together as far from the searching tendril as they possibly could be. Some were merely frightened; others had been injured in the mad scramble to get away.

As she was now the only person standing in the middle of the room, the vein soon came slithering over towards Eleri. It passed over her, starting at the outside of one foot, and travelled up her body and back down the other leg. Eleri made a face as the strange, rubbery texture of the vein moved over her face.

After it had assessed that there was a person there, the Heaving Heart's vein reared back. It did so in preparation to attempt another assault on its target's ribs, seemingly unconcerned that it was a new person.

Before it could strike, though, Eleri tossed something behind it. The item bounced noisily along the cavern floor. In the dim firelight, Sioned could just make out the shape of it from where she sat. It was one of the gryms Eleri carried, full of crystallized magic.

The vein darted after it and absorbed it fully the moment they touched.

Eleri, not waiting for anything after seeing the vein loop back around, dashed towards her friends. She tugged them from the cavern and up the tunnel; the pounding of the Heaving Heart obscured for the first time by the sounds of the Elders and attendants retreating behind them.

Chapter Twenty-Two

Eleri, Clara, and Sioned were left sitting in Alphius' study. The three of them had been ushered in there the moment the door to the secret tunnel shut behind them. Alphius and the other Elders had seemed distractedly irritated with them and refused to answer any questions. After Alphius had directed them inside his study, he had told them to wait while he finished some tasks, then shut and locked the door behind him.

Sioned and Clara had dragged two chairs close to the fireplace—which Clara then lit—and huddled as close as the furniture would allow. Both looked pale and miserable, with a shocked look about their eyes. Clara, in particular, looked haunted and kept rubbing at the spot on her chest the vein would have punctured.

Eleri, on the other hand, paced furiously. She was silent—she didn't mutter under her breath, and even her footsteps were hushed—but the air around her was charged with tension. Eleri's blue eyes were stormy, and her jaw was set like stone.

When the door finally opened, Eleri whirled on Alphius. He held up a hand to try to quell her fury, but it was in vain. Just as Eleri opened her mouth, Alphius cut her off, though he was only able to by the volume of his words.

"I don't want to hear it. The damage you have done today may be irreversible. You ought to be groveling for forgiveness."

Alphius' voice was hard with anger, and it was so loud that it seemed to bounce off the walls of the study. Eleri, already halfway through making a sound, devolved into flabbergasted sputters. She pointed a finger at him, rings glinting in the fire light, and advanced menacingly on the old man.

"You! You want to speak of forgiveness? You who tried to kill my friend only hours earlier? The absolute *audacity* that you must possess, Alphius, to think whatever plans you may have would matter more to me than the life of someone I care for."

By the time she had gotten to the end of what she was saying, Eleri stood in Alphius' personal space, jabbing her finger into his chest. He grabbed her by the wrist and wrenched her hand away, but Eleri did not flinch even though it hurt.

"You have no idea what you're talking about," Alphius snapped.

Eleri rolled her eyes, still cool and collected despite her rage and the awkward angle at which Alphius held her arm.

"That would have more meaning if it didn't come from the man I already asked for clarification and who refused to give it. You reap what you sow."

Alphius' face turned purple and spasmed with rage. He shook Eleri by the arm he was holding but let go and stepped back when it looked like Eleri was about to throw a punch. He brushed the front of his robes off, not just where Eleri had poked him, but also where dirt and dust from cowering on the cavern floor had accumulated.

"Very well, then," Alphius said, aiming for an air of wisdom, but coming across as pompous. "I would not trust you with this information normally, due to your age and immaturity—"

"Obviously you wouldn't." Eleri rolled her eyes.

"Hush! But you have meddled enough that it is now prudent to tell you of the forces you're playing with."

Alphius took a seat at his desk with an absurd amount of pomp. Sioned and Clara scooted their chairs a little closer, although they still looked shaken. Eleri remained standing, her arms crossed over her chest, staring Alphius down in stony silence.

"What you just saw is known as the Heaving Heart," Alphius began with some gravitas. "It first appeared a century ago and has been growing in size ever since. As fewer and fewer mages are born, it gains power, which leads us to believe it is a result of the Great Corruption."

"How does that equal trying to kill Clara?" Sioned broke in, her voice loud but brittle. She held Clara's hand tightly in her own.

"There is nothing that can be done to get rid of the Heaving Heart. We Elders have been trying since long before you were born. It seems to suck the very magic out of the air—no magic used against it can land, it is only absorbed. It also cannot be destroyed by regular weapons—it simply heals itself immediately."

Alphius was truly warming to his topic, gearing up for a lecture. Eleri impatiently gestured at him to get on with it.

"The only way to slow its growth that we've found is to give it regular injections of magic. When a poor soul comes to us looking for a way to give their power up, we feed it to the Heaving Heart."

Alphius said it like it was the simplest explanation.

"And that means I die?" Clara, asked, disgusted and dismayed.

Alphius shrugged.

"Anyone looking to give up their magic must be an outcast in society, so they are not missed. Wouldn't you appreciate doing something *good* for once in your life?"

Eleri picked up a letter opener from Alphius' desk and threw it. It passed by his temple by a narrow margin and embedded itself in the thick tapestry hanging behind him. Alphius jumped violently and brought his hand to his head, repeatedly touching his temple as if to check for blood. There was none.

"Perhaps I should have thrown that a little to the left, so that you could do something good for once." Eleri told him nastily through clenched teeth.

She was still standing stiff with rage, ready to face Alphius down as he rounded his desk towards her. Even so, it was obvious the night was beginning to wear in her, as her face was ashen and exhausted looking.

"You think you have any right to this land? To decide its fate? Your father may have been a king, once, but you are the princess of *naught*, little girl," the old man snarled.

Sioned and Clara jumped up from their chairs and did their best to quickly shuffle Eleri from the study before she could respond to that. She went with them, mostly willingly, though she did drag her feet somewhat and kept turning back to look at Alphius. It seemed like she had more to say, but the hands of her friends on her shoulders kept Eleri moving forward. Alphius obviously took Eleri's forced exit as a surrender and gazed at her smugly as she was ushered out.

As soon as the door was shut behind them, Eleri stopped. She tilted her head back, eyes closed, and breathed deeply through her nose. She let the breath out through her mouth, drawing out the exhale. When she looked at Sioned and Clara, her eyes were bright with anger.

"I want the two of you to go to my room, lock the door, and not let anyone in," Eleri told them, very seriously. "There is something I need to do; please stay safe until I can return."

With that, Eleri strode off down the hall, walking silently but with purpose. Unsure of her motivations, Clara and Sioned did as she bade them. Careful to avoid the other occupants of the Keep, they made their way to Eleri's room. After locking the door, both physically and with magic, they jammed a chair against it for an added measure of protection. Then, exhausted by the late night and their fright, Sioned and Clara tucked themselves in together in Eleri's narrow little bed. There they slept, wrapped in each other's arms, as Eleri made her way of the Keep and into the dark woods surrounding it, her destination clear in her mind.

The water of the lake was a clear blue when Eleri found it, more like an artist's rendition than reality. It seemed fitting, given the legendary history of the place. Eleri stood at the edge of the impossible water, her eyes trained on the hazy outline of the island before her. Even looking at it prompted a swell of magic, a subtle redirection that made focusing on the island difficult. Calling the landmass a mountain seemed a little pretentious—though large, it didn't quite *tower* the way one might expect a mountain to—but its significance made calling it a hill feel almost disrespectful. It was still mostly dark out and the stars twinkled distantly in the sky.

Here, Eleri laid eyes on the last resting place of Arthur Pendragon for the first time. Fine mist rolled off the lake and partially obscured the view. Still, the remains of what had once been an elegant tower were still visible, though it was mostly reduced to a few meagre stones. Something about the area felt like it was holding its breath, waiting. Like any minute something would happen, the music would start playing, the sky would open up and rain, the battle would begin.

The beloved king would return to his people.

It almost felt like a sin to disturb the anticipatory peace. Nevertheless, Eleri removed her cloak and boots, and had folded the fabric as if in a ceremony. She also removed her socks and stuffed them into the toes of her boots for safekeeping. Her tunic and leggings did nothing to ward off the early morning chill and her feet were already growing numb, but Eleri knew the feeling was nothing compared to what was coming. The water rippled around her legs as she stepped in, an aberration in the otherwise glassy water.

With a deep breath, she strode confidently forward until she came to the drop-off, and then dove in headfirst. The frigid temperature stole the breath from her lungs, but Eleri did not falter. With strong strokes, she swam in the direction of the island in the centre of the lake. Several times, she felt the magic around her try to push her off-course, but Eleri stubbornly swam through it.

When she pulled herself onto the island, more exhausted than a swim of that length should have left her, Eleri took a moment to catch her breath. But she was unable to rest for long, the urgency of her mission spurning her forward. Weakened, she stumbled through the ruins towards her destination.

The 'tomb' of the Once and Future King was not, in fact, a tomb. There was no body laying beneath the soil, but the monument had been erected in his honour. It had served as a place of remembrance for the king's loved ones during their lifetimes while his body rested in Avalon. Now, his daughter, heir presumptive to his weighty legacy, knelt in front of the awe-inspiring statue.

The marble man was magnificent; power radiated from him, despite the lifelessness of the medium. He looked as caring as he was strong, wise, and decisive. He was handsome, with a neat beard and dressed in simple chainmail and armour. Before him, Eleri felt more inadequate than she ever had in her life. The King was posed with his sword in his hands; the tip of Excalibur's sheath was resting against the ground and his hands folded together over the pommel. The sword itself was half drawn allowing Eleri to see that the phrase *Take Me Up* was etched into the blade.

From her place at his feet, Eleri looked up at the face of the statue. For a brief moment, questions flashed through her mind— *Do we look alike? Would he recognise me by my face, or even want to know me?*—but she put them aside. There were more important things to worry about now.

Eleri bent low, her forehead touching the tips of the stone boots. Even if it was impersonal stone, she couldn't bear to look the man in the face when asking for his assistance.

"Father—King Arthur," she began nervously, then swallowed hard around the lump in her throat. "I know I was neither a planned nor wanted child, nor could I ever live up to the standards you set, but I come to you, humble and afraid, to ask for your intercession."

Eleri paused and licked her lips. It felt strange to be talking to a statue, unsure if the man it represented could hear her wherever he was, but she had nowhere else to turn.

"If there is some way I might use Excalibur, if you could speak to the Lady of the Lake on my behalf... I am not worthy, my King, I know that. I only ask the use of Excalibur to save my friends, to save my country. The Heaving Heart cannot be defeated by spells or mortal weapons, but I cannot allow it to continue consuming mages and magic alike.

"Please..." Eleri said, brokenly. "Let me do good, give me the tool I need to help."

There was silence. Eleri's eyes were still trained on the plinth beneath the statue's feet, but she couldn't sense a change in the atmosphere. There was only the biting wind, which made her shiver in her wet clothing. The sun was starting to rise, its pale light doing nothing to warm Eleri. For a few seconds more Eleri knelt there, but there was no answer to her plea. Tears came unbidden to her eyes as her feelings of helplessness grew.

Eleri made to stand, feeling sick with rejection even though she had not truly expected to be given the honour of wielding Excalibur.

She reached out, intending to use the statue's scabbard to help pull herself up, but her hand closed around warmed leather instead of cold hard stone. Eleri looked up in surprise and awe. What she saw was the same statue as before, King Arthur's expression unchanged, except that the sword he held was now truly Excalibur.

Eleir scrambled to her feet. With trembling hands, she reached for the sword. It slid from the statue's hands with ease, and then she held Excalibur in her hands. It thrummed, not exactly with power but with some significance. Reverently, she attached its scabbard to her belt, where her own sword usually rested. It was heavier and longer than the blade Eleri favoured, but Eleri was sure she could still use it deftly.

She took a step, as if to go, but then turned back to the statue with renewed determination. Eleri climbed onto the plinth and crowded against the statue. She raised herself onto her tiptoes and placed a gentle kiss against the stone Arthur's jawline.

"Thank you, Father. If I can't make you proud, I will at least ensure you still have a land to return to."

With that, Eleri turned firmly in the direction of Gryphon's Keep. There was work to be done.

Chapter Twenty-Three

The cool underground air of the tunnel beneath the Keep was refreshing after the exertion Eleri had put herself though. From the moment she left Lake Avalon to the second she crossed the threshold of Gryphon's Keep, she had pushed herself to maintain her pace. Eleri's chest was tight, she was panting, and her face was flushed a bright pink.

She was still rushing. In her haste, Eleri had not been subtle in her return, and she knew Alphius and the other Elders would have been notified by now. There was no time to catch her breath, though she did do some breathing exercises as she ran, to try to return her lungs to normal.

Eleri stopped short at the entrance of the cavern. The pounding of the Heaving Heart drilled into her skull, and her overtaxed body quickly developed a headache pounding in tandem. Eleri felt vaguely ill, not just physically but also at the knowledge of the risk to come.

Out of habit, she rested her hand on the hilt of the sword at her waist. It was not the familiar grip of her own blade, but the handle of Excalibur was warm to the touch, as if it had just been in another's hand. It gave her comfort, not the usual reassurance of her own ability to assure her safety but the new sense of worthiness that came from being trusted with the legendary weapon.

With a new sense of calm, Eleri stepped into the cavern. The heartbeat surrounding her stuttered a moment. It threw Eleri off enough that she looked around instead of charging straight into the Heaving Heart's chamber. In the lofts above the dais, Alphius and several other Elders—mostly the ones from Clara's failed murder—stood staring down at Eleri stoically. She stood in the centre, unafraid of what they had to say.

"Evening, Elders," Eleri greeted in a pleasant voice. "I must admit to being surprised at this welcoming committee."

"We've been waiting here for you since the moment you left the Keep. I knew we couldn't trust you to keep from meddling, especially after what you saw," Alphius said; it was lucky he had such a booming voice, otherwise it may have been difficult to hear him.

Eleri made sure to project her words.

"After I saw you try to sacrifice my friend? No, I don't suppose there was any way I would be able to let that one go." Then Eleri put her index finger to the corner of her mouth in a mock-thinking pose. "Perhaps you ought to thank me for being so efficient. You could have been waiting here a long time if I hadn't returned so soon."

Alphius growled and raised a hand in a signal. From the shadows on either side of Eleri, initiates leapt forwards and grabbed her. One of them was Marcus, who leered at her as he wrapped his arms around her waist and lifted her bodily off the floor. The other, who Eleri didn't care to recognise, held her wrists together awkwardly by her left shoulder.

As soon as Eleri's feet left the ground, she started kicking. The way Marcus and the other initiates were positioned made it very unlikely she'd be able to connect with them, but Eleri hoped she could at least unbalance her captors, thinking it would be easier to escape if they were all lying on the ground.

"Enough!" Alphius shouted. "You should feel lucky we didn't just let you sacrifice yourself to the Heaving Heart with this foolish plan of yours."

"I mean, really," said another Elder. "Alphius said he told you no mere weapon could ever injure it."

"Well, we're keeping her around to study her latent magic, not her brains," laughed a third Elder, sneering down at Eleri.

This whole time, Eleri had been doing her best to ignore the jeers and work on getting free. This unseated Excalibur's sheath from her belt, and Eleri watched, horrified, as it clattered to the stone floor. This knocked the blade slightly loose from its scabbard, and Eleri could see the firelight glinting off the polished steel. The Heaving Heart stuttered again.

Eleri was half-carried, half-dragged from the entrance to the middle of the cavern. When Marcus attempted to set her on her feet again, she allowed it. Then she glared resolutely up at Alphius and the others. Alphius opened his mouth, but Eleri cut him off before he could get even a sound out.

"Please. It doesn't have to be this way; instead of feeding into the Corruption to stave off its effects, let's work together to put an end to all this suffering." The other initiate's grip had loosened, and Eleri freed her hand, lifting it up in offering to the Elders. Her voice was pleading. "Take my hand; we can rebuild, not just prolong the end."

Alphius and the other Elders laughed in chorus.

"You are a naive child! We must preserve the way of Gryphon's Keep at any cost!" scoffed a woman.

Marcus went to grab Eleri again. This time, she was expecting it, and spun out of reach. The other initiate was caught off guard by this manoeuvre, and stumbled back, tripping over the scabbard on the floor. This set the blade fully free, and it skittered over the stone until it was right by the entrance to the Heaving Heart's chamber. There was a moment of deathly silence, then the heart began pounding again with a heretofore unheard-of urgency.

"Excalibur!" Eleri cried, reaching for her father's sword.

"Excalibur?" Alphius demanded, whipping around to get a good look at the legendary weapon.

In that moment, the veins of the Heaving Heart burst through the curtain and into the main chamber. The wall, carved into the thick stone itself, was no match for the power of the Heaving Heart; it all but shattered leaving the view into the other chamber unobstructed. Shredded fabric from the curtain fluttered to the ground pathetically, and the sound of the heartbeat, still unusually fast, reverberated around the cavern. Several people shrieked in surprise.

Each of the veins dove for a different person. Marcus let go of Eleri, pushing her towards the incoming tendril to save himself. She stumbled to her knees and, as the vein darted above her head and crashed into the floor where she had just been standing, Eleri crawled to Excalibur and resheathed it.

Many of the other Elders had not been as lucky as Eleri, Marcus, or Alphius. Their bodies slumped to the floor as the victorious veins withdrew, gaping holes in their chests where their hearts used to be. Those that *had* managed to dodge the first attack had little time to recover their senses. The Heaving Heart struck out again. With little space to move, Eleri brought the scabbard to her chest and curled protectively around Excalibur, the sword clutched to her chest. Luckily, the veins gave Eleri a wide berth.

"How could this happen?" Alphius demanded, terrified and crouching behind the stone railing he'd just been using as a podium. "We have faithfully tended to the Heaving Heart since—" The rest of his sentence was lost in a gurgle. The sound of his voice appeared to have indicated his position to the Heaving Heart, and a vein pierced him in the back, ripping out his heart.

Now Eleri was alone in the carnage. Blood and bodies surrounded her, the veins undulating on the floor, ceiling, and in the air around her, though their onslaught was paused. Curious, cautious, Eleri uncurled and looked around her. She brought herself carefully to her feet.

As she stood, Eleri went to return the scabbard to her belt. As soon as Excalibur was out of the way, a vein darted forward. Eleri, quick but not quick enough to draw the sword, managed to block the attack. The vein bounced off the scabbard and recoiled as if it had been struck by the blade itself. A different vein took the place of the one that retreated, hovering around Eleri.

Eleri drew Excalibur and brought the blade up in a guard position. Only fumbling a little, Eleri quickly reattached Excalibur's sheath to her belt with one hand. Then, with careful, measured steps—and facing the Heaving Heart the entire time—Eleri brought herself to face her foe.

The Heaving Heart had grown since she'd last seen it. There were cracks in the cave walls where it pressed up against them, now too big for its chamber. The heart was now a bright, fresh red, like newly-spilled blood, but the dark, infection-like streaks had grown in size and number. It still beat furiously, and now that she had seen its aversion to Excalibur, Eleri knew it was out of fear.

Eleri gave the heart a grim smile. The reaction Excalibur had brought about made her more confident in her plan.

Now that Excalibur was directly in front of the Heaving Heart, it beat faster still. The veins spread sinuously around the cavern, looking for more victims. They almost seemed to sniff around the dead bodies like a dog, but there was no one left except for Eleri.

"Looking for more mages to fuel your power, are we?" Eleri asked, giving the sword a little twirl. It both allowed her to check how it was balanced, and to bring it into proper position.

The Heaving Heart slowly rotated towards Eleri; now it faced only her, and even seemed to be sizing Eleri up. The veins retracted until they were all undulating in the air around the heart.

Determined, Eleri took a step forward. Immediately, one of the veins lunged for her. Eleri deftly sidestepped and brought Excalibur down on the vein. The severed end hit the floor with a meaty thud. Eleri, unwilling to take her eyes off the Heaving Heart fully, watched it seize up strangely, as if it was turning to rock or bone, from the corner of her eye. Then cracks appeared across the surface, and the severed vein crumbled into black dust.

Eleri toed at the pile of dust. A few of the other veins came forward to poke at it as well, but quickly retreated—evidently unwilling to be so close to the blade that had wrought such damage. A sharp grin spread across her face, showing off her crooked canine. She brought Excalibur forward, one hand on its hilt and the other resting against the blade, showing it off.

"I know you know what this is," Eleri told the Heart. "Bearing Excalibur makes me immune to magic... And *you* are made from corrupted magic. You are right to fear it."

Eleri gave Excalibur another twirl, this time for flair rather than practicality.

"I am Eleri Pendragon, daughter of King Arthur. I have earned the right to wield this blade, not to rule over this land but as its protector. You should fear me too."

With that, Eleri ran forward. She ducked under the veins the Heaving Heart sent out, swiping at them with Excalibur. As she closed in on the heart, the veins began swinging more violently. There was less finesse behind their movements, and more power. The wild actions of the veins brought them closer than ever before, and Eleri was able to sever more of them with Excalibur. Soon, the floor was coated in the fine black powder of the disintegrated veins. Just as Eleri was closing in on the Heaving Heart, one of its veins managed to catch her in the midsection, pushing her back. It only took a moment for her to regain her wits and cut the vein in two, but it was enough to put her out of striking distance of the Heart itself.

Eleri took a steadying breath, and pain shot through her chest. She was unsure if it was caused by breathing in all the strange black dust or from the force of the blow she's just endured. Eleri put it out of her mind; pain meant nothing in the face of her goal. Again, she pushed forward.

A vein Eleri had not seen had crept forward, low to the ground, and swiped at Eleri's feet. She toppled over, landing hard on her left arm, but managed to use the momentum to bring Excalibur around and drive it into the vein. It flailed for a second or two, pinned as it was to the floor by the blade running through it, and then fell limp to the ground.

Like the others, it ossified, but this vein did not turn to dust. Nor did it move again. A quick glance around, mostly to judge how long before the next attack, revealed that only the severed tendrils disintegrated, while those that had been merely stabbed had hardened and lay useless on the ground.

Eleri made to rise and felt her left shoulder seize and give out. She crashed back to the ground, scraping her chin along the stone floor. She cursed, blood dripping from her face to the floor. Even before attempting to push herself up again, Eleri knew it was a lost cause. The sting from the Water Leaper had not fully healed, and the exertion had been too much for her already overtaxed shoulder muscles.

Her fall did not go unnoticed by the Heaving Heart. As she shifted weight to her right arm only, Eleri saw the remaining veins converge on the one she'd just stabbed. Though careful to avoid contact with Excalibur, the veins converged and began dragging both the sword and the damaged vein away.

Eleri felt her blood run cold. Her grimy face paled, and then she set her jaw in determination. Eleri hauled her body forward with just her good arm, until she could get her feet under her. Her right ankle protested her weight, evidently injured by her fall as well, but Eleri again ignored the pain.

Eleri had not fully risen before she threw herself at the retreating veins. She grabbed for Excalibur but did not have the height to reach for the handle. Her hands closed around the blade, the sharpened edges biting into the flesh of her palms. She grit her teeth, sucking in a harsh breath through the pain, but refused to let go.

"This is my *father's* sword; it was entrusted to me. I will not lose it, and I will not leave my friends in danger," Eleri ground out, slowly hauling herself up the blade of Excalibur, hand over hand. This also helped bring her fully to her feet.

When her right hand closed around the handle of the sword, Eleri all but ripped it from the vein. She stood for a moment, chest heaving and breath ragged—little wheezes sometimes breaking through. Blood dripped from her chin and her hands, she was filthy with dirt, dust, and the remains of the veins. Eleri kept her weight to her left leg, which made her unresponsive left arm hang limply by her side. Her hair, which had still been damp at the beginning of the fight, was tangled and matted, the waves wild and partly obscuring her face. The little blue ribbons hung limp and half-untied from the dark strands. The one eye that was visible practically glowed a near electric blue as Eleri's magic surged through her body.

Eleri twirled Excalibur, finding her grip again. With slow, even, and deliberate steps, she advanced on the Heaving Heart. Again, the heart tried to repel her with its veins, but Eleri systematically cut off all tendrils that came close to her. The beat of the Heaving Heart sped up, clearly terrified. As she approached, Eleri kicked some of the hardened veins from her path but did not slow down. When she was close to the heart again, it tried to sweep her away like it had the first time, but Eleri knew that trick. She easily sliced off the offending vein before it could make contact with her chest.

"You've done enough damage," Eleri told the Heaving Heart simply. "It's time to start rebuilding."

With that, Eleri drove Excalibur through the muscle of the heart, throwing all her weight behind it, right beneath where the ventricles were located. The Heaving Heart beat once, twice, then began to solidify like the veins. With a resounding crack, faults began to form along the stony surface of the heart, and then it suddenly collapsed into a pile of dust.

Eleri collapsed with it now that there was no resistance to hold Excalibur in place. Exhausted, damp, and in pain, Eleri managed to stumble her way over to the wall of the cavern. There she sat, her back resting against the stone, right leg extended and left folded up by her chest. Excalibur lay by her side, still held loosely in her grip. Eleri tilted her head back to rest against the wall, struggling to catch her breath, and closed her eyes. A little rest was well deserved.

Chapter Twenty-Four

Springtime came to Gryphon's Keep slowly. The ground warmed, and the grass came back to green. Little pops of colour started appearing as flowers began to bud and then bloom. As life returned to the world around them, so, too, did the inhabitants of the Keep become rejuvenated.

The winter had been long and cold. A fine layer of snow had occasionally dusted the grounds, but it was mostly heavy rain that kept them inside the Keep. On days when the rain was very intense, or a thunderstorm rolled in, the three women brought their individual tasks to the library and sat around the roaring fire together. Even with the magic that was so ingrained in the stone walls, it could be cold and drafty in the Keep.

But there was plenty of work to keep them busy. Sioned, with a head for numbers, went over the records of expenses from the last handful of years. Eleri worked to sort the research that had been done and learned to control her own budding abilities. Clara used the initiates that still remained to keep Gryphon's Keep running, even if it was just the basic functionality.

Slowly, they rebuilt Gryphon's Keep from the inside out. With the Heaving Heart now destroyed, Eleri was hopeful the magic it had hoarded would return to the world, and that Excalibur would have purified it. With less of a reason to ration magic and commandeer all new mages, it was her dream that the Keep would return to being an institution of learning and community, rather than an iron-fisted regulatory body.

On the first day of spring, Eleri, Clara, and Sioned had brought out a blanket and took their lunch as a picnic. It was a dry day with no sign of rain, and the sun shone weakly but warmly on them. Clara helped herself to another scone while Sioned tilted her head back, sunning herself. They had accomplished much over the past few months and were treating their first meal outdoors like a little celebration.

Eleri, who was laying on her front reading a book, hummed slightly. When the other two turned to look at her, she gave a little laugh.

"I'd almost forgotten. It's my birthday today."

"What?" Sioned exclaimed. "Why didn't you mention this before?"

Clara even reached out to swat at Eleri's shoulder lightly.

"It's never really been something I celebrate, you know. My mother certainly wasn't pleased by my birth, and there was no one who wanted me when I was young." Eleri rolled over to look directly at her friends. Her expression was light, but thoughtful. "I believe this is the first year I would have had someone to celebrate with, with you two."

"I wish you would have said something," Sioned grumbled. "We could have had a proper celebration."

"I usually dread it. It's a reminder of how I came into this world, and how I was meant to leave it early. The fact that I forgot it was approaching, and that I am not spending today miserable is enough for me."

Eleri, still laying on her back, was surprised when Clara jumped to her feet.

"But it's not enough for me! We'll have the kitchen make you a cake, at least."

Still on her back, Eleri gave an approximation of a shrug, a little smile on her face. She held a hand out, and Clara rolled her eyes but used it to pull Eleri to her feet.

"A cake would be lovely, though not necessary. Make it one to celebrate all the hard work we've been doing." Eleri brushed off her tunic, although there was nothing really on it. It was a way to avoid looking at Clara, which Eleri gladly took.

When she could pretend to dust herself off no more, Eleri looked back at Clara. Sioned had stood and joined her, and they were both looking at Eleri with a fond but troubled look. Before either of them could say anything, Eleri rushed to speak.

"I think I'll head back to Avalon tomorrow." She wrapped a gentle hand around the hilt of Excalibur and ran her thumb back and forth over the pommel.

"What? Why?" Sioned demanded.

She grabbed Eleri's elbow, as if to keep her in place. Eleri didn't fight it but did look at Sioned curiously.

"I need to return Excalibur to my father. I was never meant to keep it," Eleri explained. "It won't take me very long; I should be back the day after tomorrow at the latest."

"You don't have to go," Sioned said.

"I promised my father I'd return it; that's how I won the right to wield Excalibur, however briefly."

"Your father, your father!" Sioned exploded. "You are talking about a *statue*!"

"I know," Eleri said quietly, looking down. "But it's all I have of him."

There was a moment of uncomfortable silence. Eleri then turned to leave, pausing only to pick up her book from the picnic blanket. She hadn't gotten far when Clara called out to her, though Eleri did not turn around.

"I think you're worthy, you know. It doesn't matter to me what some stupid sword or statue thinks."

After Eleri had retreated inside the Keep, Clara sat down again with a sigh. Sioned did, too, and pressed close to Clara's side. She rested her head on Clara's shoulder.

"It's hard, you know. To grow up feeling alienated from your family. I get why Eleri wants something that feels like parental love." Clara sounded tired and world-weary.

Sioned gave Clara's cheek a light kiss.

"Come home with me," Sioned said impulsively.

"What?" Clara asked, jostling Sioned in her surprise.

"Come home with me," Sioned repeated. "My family has always known I'd settle down with a woman, and I'm sure they'd love you. We can continue our work here, but also build a new life for the two of us."

Clara's face fell. She grabbed onto Sioned's hand and gripped it tight.

"My family won't be happy. They'll treat you terribly." Clara gave a humourless laugh. "Maybe even worse than they treat me."

Sioned spun to face Clara, their hands still connected. Her face had a fiercer expression on it than Clara had ever seen.

"We don't need them. Run away with me. I will love you as you are, and my family will, too. Or we can run away again." Suddenly, Sioned's expression dropped into something softer. "I almost lost you, so soon after finding you. I won't settle for a future without you by my side—and I want you as happy as can be in it."

Sioned reached up and gently thumbed away the tears from Clara's face. She hadn't even realised she was crying until that moment. Clara put her hand over Sioned's, where it rested on her cheek, and smiled at her partner.

"I only want a future with you, too, no matter what it looks like."

They spent the rest of the afternoon planning their visit to Sioned's family estate, and how to divide their time between their responsibilities at Gryphon's Keep and their own burgeoning relationship. Lost in their own little world, they didn't notice when Eleri left in the morning.

The scenery around Lake Avalon was beautiful, Eleri noted, now that she had the time to appreciate it. She sat on the edge of the lake with her bare toes in the water, sometimes splashing a little. Excalibur, still in its scabbard, had been unpinned from her belt and rested at her side. She kept a ready hand on it—either out of preparedness, or as a source of strength. Her gaze was distant, fixed unseeingly on the island and its ruins.

Eleri had been sitting there for quite some time. She had travelled leisurely to the lake after breakfast, meandering along the way, and had lunched on cheese, bread, and a juicy plum while sitting on the shoreline. Even after all the stickiness had been licked from her fingers, Eleri did not get up to do what she had come for.

The sky was covered by soft grey clouds threatening rain, but Eleri was still warm enough in her tunic. It was marginally nicer than her last visit, possibly owing to the later hour of the day. It wasn't, however, a reluctance towards the icy swim that kept Eleri from the water.

No, instead it was the realisation that she was now at the end of the only sort of interaction with her father she'd ever get that kept Eleri from diving in. The spectre of King Arthur had loomed over her since the moment of her conception, his legend defining and overshadowing the entirety of Eleri's existence. In spite of all this, she felt a strong pull towards him. Eleri both yearned for his love and approval, and desired to cast off the Pendragon shadow completely.

Wielding Excalibur had offered a sense of belonging to her father, and of being a worthy heir. Eleri had promised that it was for a limited time—if she didn't want to prove herself as unworthy as she had always been called, she needed to return it. Even though doing so meant giving up the only thing of her father she ever had, aside from the blood in her veins. Besides, with the defeat of the Heaving Heart, there was no need for Excalibur anymore.

Eleri stood and held Excalibur in its sheath with both hands. She rested her forehead against the pommel, took a deep breath, and exhaled it slowly. After she had done that, she waded out into the water and dove beneath the surface without pause. It was easier the second time to make it to the island—not even the misdirection spells meant to keep King Arthur's resting place safe were a match for Excalibur's powers.

Eleri pulled herself onto the island shore, staining the knees of her leggings with the dewy grass. With quick strides, she made her way back through the ruins to where the statue of King Arthur stood. Even with its hands empty, hovering above where the sword used to sit strangely, it still had a regal air. She felt childish approaching it, soaking wet with green knees and tangled hair.

Eleri scrubbed at Excalibur's wet scabbard with her sleeve; it wasn't dirty, and the action did nothing to dry it off, but she wanted to show that she knew it was a poor condition to return it in. Eleri gently fit the sword back into place in the statue's grasp in the same way she had found it originally.

Nothing happened.

Feeling unsure, Eleri scuffed her toe against the overgrown grass at her feet and looked up at the carved face. When she spoke, her voice came out stronger than she felt.

"I brought Excalibur back, Father. I have fulfilled my promise and protected your lands."

Eleri stood in silence, expecting to see Excalibur turn back into stone, but it did not. After a moment, Excalibur suddenly tipped back towards Eleri, out of the statue's grip. Eleri lunged for it, catching it before the sword could hit the ground.

She held it by the scabbard and looked curiously between Excalibur and the statue of the king. Excalibur fit perfectly into its hands; there was no wiggle room that should have allowed the sword to fall out.

Suddenly, it dawned on her, and Eleri's expression hardened into one of determination. With gentle but firm hands, she refit Excalibur into the statue's hands. It fit tightly for a second, then fell into Eleri's hand again.

"I can't keep it," she told the king. "I'm not—I don't feel worthy of it. I want to do things in my own name, be myself for a while longer. I hope you understand."

Tears prickled in Eleri's eyes. She couldn't tell if they were happy tears from being offered her father's sword, or sad ones from having to turn it down. She sniffled once.

"Thank you for your faith in me. Maybe one day I can see myself as you do."

It was strange, Eleri thought, talking to the statue as if it was actually her father, but its show of faith in her brought more joy than she had ever felt before. For the first time, Eleri felt like more than a failed extension of her mother—she truly felt like a Pendragon.

Carefully, Eleri lowered Excalibur to the ground, then she ducked under the statue's arms. It was a tight and awkward position, its stone hands digging painfully into her back. Her wet tunic scrunched uncomfortably against her skin. It was impossible for her to bring her arms up, so Eleri just looped them around the statue's waist. The stone was cold where she had her cheek pressed up against it, but the approximation of paternal affection warmed Eleri's heart.

It took a little more manoeuvring to slip back out, but she managed it just fine. Eleri replaced Excalibur a third time with a stern look at the statue, and it stayed in place. The clouds parted for a moment, and a flash of light caught the words engraved into the steel: *Cast Me Away.*

"If I ever need Excalibur again, I hope you will still find me worthy, and I hope I make you proud."

With that, Eleri turned and walked away from the statue of King Arthur with her head held high. The stone man stood impassively behind her, Excalibur still real and gleaming, with daffodils blooming around its feet.